Also by the author:

SETTRIGHT ROAD, short stories, Dzanc Books 2017

THE CASTAWAY LOUNGE, novel, Dzanc Books 2015

A RIVER CLOSELY WATCHED, novel, MacAdam Cage 2013

Junk City

stories and poems

Jon Boilard

Livingston Press
The University of West Alabama
Livingston, Alabama, United States

ISBN 13: trade paper 978-1-60489-261-1
ISBN 13: hardcover 978-1-60489-262-8
ISBN 13: e-book 978-1-60489-263-5

Library of Congress Control Number 20200940004
Printed on acid-free paper
Printed in the United States of America by
Publishers Graphics

Hardcover binding by: HF Group
Typesetting and page layout: Joe Taylor
Proofreading: Maddie Owen, Tricia Taylor, Jada Baxter, Hilary Nelson,
Mike Faulkner

Cover Design: Joe Taylor

Cover & author's photograph: Leslie Edelman

Acknowledgments

These stories appeared, sometimes in different form, in the following publications: "Green Street Incidents" (*The Sun Magazine*), "Falling" (*subTerrain Magazine*), "The Good Kind" and "Small Deaths" (*Southword Journal*), "Two Rules" (*The Dalhousie Review*), "Undertow" (*Sulphur River Literary Review)*, "Fat Priest Face" (*RE:AL Journal*), "La Playa" (*Verdad Magazine*), "The Parrot" (*Lynx Eye)*, "Tormenta" (*Puerto del Sol)*, "Nothing to Lose" (*Beloit Fiction Journal*) and "Capp Street Reunion" (*Fugue*). In addition, "The Good Kind" won the Seán ó Faoláin Award in 2005.

Livingston Press is part of The University of West Alabama,
and thereby has non-profit status.
Donations are tax-deductible.
6 5 4 3 2 1

Junk City

Foreword

During the California Gold Rush of 1849, San Francisco's population grew rapidly as tens of thousands turned up to find their fortunes. Those early days were characterized by lawlessness, gambling, administrative graft, vigilante justice, and prostitution. The Barbary Coast district was the sordid capital of the city, but over time the local government put its foot down and San Francisco in due course became known more for its majestic views and five-star food than its skullduggery. Flash forward to 2019 and a new gold rush is upon us, with tech titans setting up world headquarters South of Market and tapping an international talent pool whose members arrived in the Bay Area on electronic scooters to take over entire neighborhoods. These modern-day speculators don cotton hoodies, ballerina jeans, and Jesus sandals, but like the forty-niners of old, they too mean to strike it rich quick. For all its beauty and despite the influx of astounding volumes of wealth, the city maintains a gritty underbelly that evokes the erstwhile Barbary Coast. You can find it in the shadows of the Salesforce Tower if you look hard enough. Some days you don't have to look very hard at all.

CONTENTS

(Eskimo's poems are in italics)

This one is for Chelsea

“When you pass through the waters, I will be with you; and through the rivers, they shall not overwhelm you; when you walk through fire you shall not be burned, and the flame shall not consume you.” — *Isaiah 43:2*

FINDING ALBERT REDWINE

I smoked crack before they called it that. This was San Francisco in the 1980s. I had a good job delivering the mail and a house that I shared with my Marine buddy Danny. We hated the Lakers more than anything and were throwing a party to celebrate another Celtics victory. Larry Bird got a triple double and he was like a god. It was mostly guys from the post office and the West Sunset basketball courts where we played pickup. There were always some pretty ladies around. I got so fucked up I couldn't even stand.

People were starting to leave because it was late, and it was Wednesday. Danny's kid sister tried to pull me off the couch. Her name was Beth and sometimes I called her Betty Boop after that cartoon. She had a thing for me and so I was nailing her behind Danny's back. It started by accident and then I couldn't stop. If he found out, then we would have to fight. He was Golden Gloves, but I don't know who would've won because I'd been in my share of scraps, too. In the Corp nobody messed with either of us.

It was wrong of me yet most of what I did was wrong. She was old enough so that it was legal but still. Danny was face down in the kitchen where he puked. Beth sneaked us into my bedroom. I begged her to leave me alone but once she took off her clothes it was all over. She had bleach-blond hair cropped short. I broke up with her last Christmas and she tried to overdose. That night in the back of the ambulance on the way to the hospital so they could pump her stomach she told me next time she'd do it right. I held her hand but only because I didn't know what to say. She told me I could never leave her. After that incident the sex was always violent and exhausting and beautiful. I usually felt bad about it. She was petite and sometimes I called her the featherweight champ.

***

I was walking my route. There was that fog-haze hiding the sun a bit. I wasn't supposed to find him. His name was Albert Redwine. His garage door was open, and I needed a signature, so I went inside. He didn't own a dog, that much I knew. I said his name two or three times. Then he was swinging there in a little breeze. He'd used an orange extension cord looped over a ceiling beam and his face was puffy and blue, his neck swollen around the cord. I didn't know what to make of it because I had never seen a dead person before. Not outside a funeral home. Even in the Corp we got gypped out of any action. Too young for Vietnam and too old for Bosnia. I sat on an overturned bucket, probably the one he had used to get himself into position. Jesus Christ. It really got to me.

He didn't leave any note in an obvious place. His mail was mostly bills and the package that required his signature was from Juneau, Alaska. It smelled like he'd shit his pants and I'd heard about how that would happen when your body shuts down. Other than that, he was tidy, and his jeans were creased in the middle. There were goose bumps on my forearms. I didn't know what could make a person go through all the trouble. He must have had a plan. His eyes were open and looking at me as though in judgment.

***

The Lakers beat the Celtics in game four and Danny smashed

the television in the street. Alejandro was wearing a Magic Johnson t-shirt and so Danny busted his lip. Somebody pulled a gun until the cops showed up and stuck Danny in the paddy wagon. Beth cleaned up the house a little. I pretended to be asleep, but she was smarter than that. I told her about finding Albert Redwine and she wondered what it felt like, so I put my hands around her neck, and I squeezed her windpipe although not too much. Beth was scared but got on top of me so I could see her emptying eyes by the trembling light of a candle.

needles

yesterday
believing
a dreamer need not weep

thunder slumber

pillow hair
moon scarred eyes cry
sleepskin shudders
cuddled in uncomfort
panic grimly steeps

gnashing nurture
fork tongue torture
blinding shadows reap
hell less hounds
mouthless sounds
fatal hours creep

midnight serving
pain deserving

sweat scabbed

bloodshot
heap
~ eskimo

SAYING SUCH DON'T MAKE IT SO

There's a dancer from Little Darlings at the bar drinking a vodka soda through a red stirring straw. Joxer sits next to her and she notices his black eye. He notices her noticing but doesn't want to get into it. He's not interested in giving her the why for of a dude suckerpunching him out on Columbus Avenue and then ending up on a gurney in an ambulance on his way to General. Fuck happened to you, she says after a few minutes.

Joxer really looks at her good for the first time. He likes what he sees.

Got hit by a bus, he says.

She laughs and sips at her drink.

A friend of mine did that once and sued the city, she says.

Well, I better get a damn lawyer.

Yeah, for real, he made like a million dollars.

Joxer wonders what a million dollars looks like. He finishes his Jack and Coke. Where you from, he says.

Alaska, originally.

She goes by Eskimo and they talk for the better part of an hour. She writes poems in her free time. Joxer doesn't know shit about poetry but he likes her because she's smart and funny and no-bullshit. He likes her because she didn't pick her stage name from the three-color car ads in the Sunday paper. He also likes her because she's beautiful. She's got to begin her shift, so he walks her to the club, and she gives him some free passes. It's one of Sloop's uncle's places. The doorman does the fucking prick act because Joxer looks like bad news, but Eskimo uses her impressive powers of persuasion to get him in. The place smells like a piece of heaven: fruity body lotion and girl sweat and pussy. The deejay introduces her as Eh, Eh, Eskimo. Joxer sits in the front row. She dances slow and sexy and sad to Johnny Cash doing his remake of *Hurt* by Nine Inch Nails and Joxer can't believe it. He loves that version. It must be some kind of fate. When she finishes her routine, she sits on his lap and rubs cocaine into his upper gums with her index finger. Where have you been all this shitty life, she whispers in his ear.

***

Two weeks later and they're at Gino & Carlo watching Mick Graham win the annual pool tournament for the third time in three years. It's the sure sign of a misspent youth, Mick always says. Growing up in billiard halls in and around Dublin. Joxer puts his glass on the bar and goes outside for a smoke. Eskimo joins him. It's her night off. They're behaving like a normal couple on some kind of date. Wind coming off the bay and rushing through the streets is making it difficult for them to light the cigarettes, but Eskimo prevails. She's a real pro. A couple teens go by on skateboards and the redhead says something stupid but Joxer ignores him because the little shit doesn't know any better. Drunks are lining up at Golden Boy's for a warm slice. Nick the Cop takes a break from walking the beat. Joxer introduces him to Eskimo. She's from Alaska, he says.

You don't look like any Eskimo I've ever seen, Nick says.

Eskimo laughs. How many have you seen, she says.

Fair point, Nick the Cop says. Well, what do you do.

What do I do.

Yeah, for money. What's your job.

She takes a long drag and blows it over her shoulder, turning her head to do it, taking her time, playing a part. Then she looks him in the eye. I'm a dancer, she says.

Nick wasn't born yesterday. He knows what that means. He figures she works at the Condor or Little Darlings on Columbus. The Hungry I. He's seen some of the exotic girls down there and she'd fit right in. He smiles at her and turns back to Joxer, wants to lecture him on fighting and drinking and drugging and hanging around with whores. He's always liked Joxer, thinks of him almost as a younger brother. But he knows preaching would fall on deaf ears at this point. Always one pretty thing or another, is what he says.

Then there's a scuffle in the pizza line. Nick the Cop pays attention, but you'd hardly notice. Rather than jump into any kind of fracas right away he prefers to let the idiots try to sort it out on their own at first. He's been doing this job a long time. And he used to be the King of the Knuckleheads in the Outer Sunset, so he understands the mentality as it were. It's going to be a full night and he wants to conserve energy.

Yeah, but this one's more than just a pretty face, Joxer says.

Nick raises his eyebrows and looks from Joxer to Eskimo and back again.

How's that, he says, halfway interested.

Joxer sucks on his cigarette for a few seconds. Blows a perfect smoke ring. She's got brains too, he says as he puts his arm around her waist. She's a motherfucking poet.

A poet, Nick thinks, touching his belt. But just saying such don't make it so. It's a line he got from his grandmother, rest in peace. He always took it to mean talk is cheap.

He looks again at Eskimo and now she blushes, flips

her hair back. She's wearing lipstick and eye shadow, but she doesn't need any kind of makeup. Not with that face. Well, Nick knows lots of poets if all you had to do was say it. Joxer tells her to recite a verse or two on the spot but she refuses. Somebody inside Gino & Carlo calls her name.

Yeah, we're getting away together, Joxer says. A new life and whatnot.

No shit.

That's right.

Well, where you going.

Up north. Russian River.

Nick isn't convinced. He looks at Eskimo. The voice in the bar calls her name.

Got to go, she says.

The pool tournament, Joxer says.

Nick nods his head. Joxer and Eskimo drop their butts and push them into the pavement and go inside. Nick the Cop waves them off just as things are getting out of hand at Golden Boy's. The fat Mexican with all the tattoos is the aggressor so Nick steps behind him and pinches his wrist. The mere sight of a uniformed cop makes the other one, a pretty boy surfer dude, back off. His girlfriend shouts obscenities. She's a total nut-job, Nick can see that right away, his goofy-radar alerting him from jump.

Shut her the fuck up, Nick the Cop tells the kid in the flip flops and jeans.

The fat Mexican is on his knees now. Resisting a little but he's starting to get the point. Nick the Cop speaks calmly into the radio clipped to his shoulder, requesting some backup and the wagon. All the iPhones are out now, everybody shooting video for posterity. Everybody wanting to make him a YouTube star. Goading him with words and chants but he ignores them, plays it straight. The girlfriend is still being a pain in the ass. Nothing an overnight stay at 850 Bryant won't cure. He gives the pretty boy another look, silently asking for help with her, telling him *shut her up already*. And the Mexican finally relaxes, clasps his fingers behind his head as though it's old hat and Nick the Cop holds his hands together there. It's almost a gentle human transaction. Jukebox music spills into Green Street. It sounds like one of those old Elvis Presley songs. *Like a river flows surely to the sea ... darling so it goes ... some things are meant to be.*

There are five pizzas on display in the window: cheese, pepperoni, three-meat, mushroom and sausage, and some sort of veggie combo. Nick the Cop can smell them. Damn it if he can't. Closes his eyes to breathe in the pies as a dented white van marked SFPD suddenly appears and growls and parks next to the red fire hydrant. Two gung-ho rookies with military crew cuts and fitness club muscles jump out before it completely stops. And the wacky girlfriend finally ceases running her pretty little potty mouth.

***

Joxer scratches on the eight ball. He apologizes to Eskimo for being such a lousy partner. Billy D and the Iranian are glad to have a win and don't really care how it came about. They're high fiving and barking like that old junkyard dog and making a big scene at the other end of the table. Playing the crowd for laughs. Joxer can't stand that kind of bush league bullshit and it takes Eskimo a few minutes to calm him down. Then she playfully steers him to the bar and Frankie Junior sets them up with a couple Jacks on the house. Joxer half sits on a stool and she stands behind him, kneading his shoulders like bread.

He puts his drink away and turns the glass over with a bang. Frankie Junior grabs it and swipes at the wet ring on the bar with a dishrag. Gets him another one, looks at Eskimo.

Those fucking guys, Joxer says.

Don't let it get to you, Frankie says, looking at Joxer now.

I know, but Jesus.

They're just assholes.

Eskimo agrees, whispering in Joxer's ear.

Don't let them wreck your night, she says.

He turns on his stool to look at her. She has glitter on her shoulders and chest.

Our night maybe, he says.

That's the ticket.

There's something about him. Eskimo hasn't felt this way about a man in a while. She has only been in town for ten months but early on she learned the legend of the Sunset Badass. Eskimo has been around violent men all her life, drunken stepfathers and abusive boyfriends, and it's true that she has a knack for dealing with them, but Joxer isn't any kind of bully. He's the other kind. A man of principle, strange as it is to say. Violence is simply how he fixes things and makes them all right for a minute or two.

Frankie Junior is in the billiard room now talking to Billy D and the Iranian. Telling them they ought to tone it down. Everybody likes to win but no need to create a spectacle. That kind of thing. At first Billy D isn't very receptive as the adrenaline from the victory is still running through his veins and puffing him up like a rooster. And the Iranian is being an even bigger prick about it. He raises his voice to a shout and tells Frankie to fuck off. Then Billy D suddenly realizes that Frankie is trying to save them. Joxer and Eskimo and everybody are watching from the bar. Of a sudden he recognizes the Sunset Badass from a scrap he had wagered on years ago; lost a few bucks betting against him, in fact. He puts his hand on his partner's forearm to quiet him down.

All right, he says.

But the Iranian is on a roll now. Feeling his oats.

Enough, Billy D says.

Says it a few times until the Iranian runs out of steam and stops his jabbering.

You're right, Frankie, Billy D says.

Frankie is happy to have gotten through to them.

I'm sorry, Billy D says.

Frankie Junior relaxes. Somebody pops quarters into the jukebox. Blue Suede Shoes. Elvis Presley. Jesus Christ. Frankie is considering removing all the Elvis from the machine. The king of rock and roll my ass, he thinks. King of giving me migraines.

Buy them a drink on us, Billy D says, waving at Joxer. He takes a few soggy bills from his pocket and hands them to Frankie Junior. And a shot for you and Steve, too.

Frankie goes back behind the bar.

There's a part of Joxer that's disappointed. He had already played it out in his mind, how it would've gone down. Wait for them in the alley out back where they probably parked illegally. Break the Iranian's jaw with a hard-right uppercut. Do it so he won't be able to spout any more nonsense for a while. Wired shut and all that. Maybe go a little easier on Billy D. Maybe. Work him with some jabs, mostly body shots, use him like a heavy bag. Soften up his kidneys and bruise a rib or two. Something to think about when he rolls out of bed in the morning. Joxer loves it for sure. The rush he gets from a random fight, from lighting people up on the spot. In the ring or in some dank basement or in the street, it's the only time in his life that he can compensate for his mistakes in the very next instant. But now he's got to have a reason other than just scratching an itch.

***

Sheila can't believe she's dating such a pussy. If you'd even call it that—only their second or third date depending on how you're counting. That wetback had grabbed her ass and Joey wasn't going to even say anything until she prodded him. She deserves a real man and tells him as much. They're walking back to his upstairs flat on Vallejo Street. She's in his face the whole time. And she still wants to go dancing. He hates dancing and he's starting to hate this psycho bitch from his sister's job at the café. The way he sees it, they're lucky the old cop let them off the hook and should call it a night.

Give it a rest, he says.

Fuck you say.

Just stop.

Shit.

It's over.

I knew you were a faggot the minute I saw you the very first time.

She goes on and on about it. How she is used to dating guys with balls. They stop in front of the heavy gated door to his building and he feels around his front pockets for his key. Can't find it at first.

See what I mean, she says.

He looks at her.

Can't even find your balls, she says. Laughs at him until he locates his key.

Joey walks up the three flights and Sheila follows him.

She's still talking shit. He recognizes that it's like foreplay to her, but he's getting a headache and doesn't even want to bone her anymore. He doesn't mind boning her, she's a decent toss, but it's everything that comes before and after that is wearing him down. So, he tunes her out as best he can. He hopes she'll get laryngitis soon. They enter his apartment. He doesn't have much furniture, just an old garage-sale couch and a television. A twin mattress and box spring in the corner. And there's an old portable stereo plugged into a wall outlet.

But the first thing you really notice is the surfboards. His personal long board is zipped up in its cover by the door so he can grab it quick in the morning, drag it down to the street, secure it to the roof of the VW van that he parks wherever he can find a spot—sometimes all the way over in Chinatown—and head out to Ocean Beach for a rip or two. Always four or five other planks that he's repairing or waxing. A couple sawhorses and a sheet of half-inch plywood that he uses as a work bench. Between his little shop and the tips he makes bar backing, he's able to cover rent, buy food and gas, and have enough left over to score some weed or get a round of drinks every now and then.

***

Nick the Cop explains drunk and disorderly to the ink-covered Mexican. He explains his right to a lawyer and to not say anything stupid or otherwise. The fog is settling around them now, almost like a light rain. One of the rookies, Buzz Padykula's son, shoves the Mexican into the van without much trouble. Four or five other passengers already. Not bad. Slow night in North Beach. Only a few stragglers out and about now. The ponytailed bouncer from Maggie's. The redheaded skater with the smart mouth. The pink haired, nose ringed girl behind the glass at Golden Boy's pulls the shutters down, bolts the door.

Nick the Cop feels okay about letting the pretty boy walk away, but he actually felt bad for the guy as his foul mouth girlfriend let him have it all the way down the street until they disappeared around the corner onto Columbus Avenue. Nick has dated some nutjobs in his day, and he sure can relate. Then he gets the other rookie, Patton or something, to do the paperwork so they can process the Mexican. He hates paperwork.

It's cause I'm brown skinneded, the Mexican says to nobody in particular.

The rookie is closing the door and Nick the Cop tells him to hold on a minute.

What's that, fucknuts, he says.

How come you let white dude walk.

No, it's not because you're brown.

The Mexican spits.

It's because you're acting like an asshole.

And what about the cracker.

He didn't act like an asshole. Think about it.

Nick smiles and slams the door shut to the protests of the Mexican. Getting the others riled up too. Good. Let them get it out of their systems now, Nick the Cop thinks. We'll see who has anything left in the tank when it's time to hand out peanut butter sandwiches, quarts of low-fat chocolate milk, bruised apples and blankets. Then it will be a different deal. Officer this and officer that. Everybody playing nice. If he's seen it once he's seen it a million times. Then that redhead with the skateboard approaches him.

Just what I need, Nick the Cop thinks. Smoking a damn cigarette underage even. He snatches the cancer stick from the redhead's lip, takes himself a long drag from it.

Hey, you can't do that, the redhead says.

Says who.

Nick the Cop flicks it into the street. The redhead scowls.

Why you busting my balls.

How old are you.

Shit. Do you know who I am.

Nick the Cop doesn't know who he is, and he doesn't really give a shit. It doesn't matter. These kids nowadays. This snowflake generation. Go home Carrot Top, he says. Red drops his skateboard wheels-down onto the sidewalk, does some fancy footwork too fast to register with the naked eye, turns and rolls away. Flips the old cop the bird.

***

Nick the Cop swims laps at the downtown YMCA every morning after his shift, otherwise he'd never be able to sleep during the day. They keep the water on the cold side, which is all right with him as he tends to run a little hot. He's in the fast lane with two Asian women that are ridiculous the way they stop and start and don't mind the most basic forms of lap swim etiquette. There's an art to doing laps in a public pool and sharing water space with random strangers of different ages and varying skill levels.

He rests in the deep end, forearm on the deck, adjusts his goggles, eyeballs the lifeguard who is half asleep in the white chair and oblivious to his charges, lets the gal in front of him get a bit of a lead so he won't swim directly up her ass. Then he pushes off the wall and about halfway down the lane he has a good rhythm going. His goal is to knock out forty to fifty minutes. His right foot is cramping up, but he ignores it.

Worse than the Asians are the Russians, he thinks. The

way they seem to feel entitled to water exercise. And the way they dominate the hot tub and dry sauna afterward. Fat bastard almost drowning in the medium fast lane adjacent accidentally claws Nick, he feels the fingernails dig into the skin of his exposed flank. Stay on your side of the line, he thinks. Jesus Christ. But he keeps his head, maintains his even breathing, focuses on his form. Checks the clock on the wall, two more laps should do it, he figures. The lifeguard is full-on snoozing now. Chin to his chest. Good way to get shit-canned, Nick the Cop thinks. I ought to report him. He stops in the shallow end, massages his foot, stretches his legs. Creepy Pete is in the slower lane, underwater, checking out the female swimmers as they flip turn, hoping to see a tit fall out or some stray pubic hairs. He's famous for that. That's his big move. He thinks nobody's onto him.

Then Nick the Cop is getting dressed in the locker room. Showered but he can't ever completely shake the smell of chlorine. Ready for a Tennessee Grill breakfast followed by a power nap. Three stools down and rolling up his yoga mat sits Timmy Three Fingers. Lost the others in an argument with a table-saw several years ago, apparently. They know each other from Saturday morning hoops in the Panhandle.

How's the yoga, Nick asks.

He likes to give Timmy shit about it, this new-age thing he's doing.

Got to try it man, Timmy says.

Yeah, maybe someday.

Timmy laughs. I'm telling you, he says.

For years you been telling me.

Good for an old body like you got.

Nick laughs. Fuck you, he says.

And the instructor today was just my type.

Oh, she had a pulse you mean.

Timmy laughs. She bends over, it's like two Twinkies pressed together, he says.

Bet it don't taste like that.

There's a rumor that Timmy is a third-rate pimp. It seems like everybody is trying to get in the game, one way or another. This clown considers himself to be a ladies' man. Nick the Cop finishes up and says so long. It's about to be rush hour in there with all the lawyers and doctors and money managers, the captains of industry, the tech bros, preparing for conference calls while running on track machines and stair climbers, like Sisyphus pushing that old rock up the hill. Outside on Steuart Street a warm breeze smells of human feces and here comes a tweaker with a head full of spiders and a Safeway shopping cart. A waiter folds white linen napkins at Perry's, singing *Bésame Mucho* under his breath. Twin red Maserati double parked half a block away, empty of drivers but engines purring. What a town, Nick thinks, shoulders his gym bag and crosses against the light at Boulevard just as a crimson sun crests the Ferry Building clock tower.

bird

some bird
sat on
what wall

some bird
some bird

sat on what wall

she sat

& flew

some bird
she flew
& flew

some bird
sat on
what wall
& flew

some bird

left nothing behind

but shit
~ eskimo

GREEN STREET INCIDENTS

I open my eyes and Carol Doda tells me to fuck off. I put my head back on the bar. Then it must be a couple hours later and I'm upstairs and it's dark and I'm thinking of quicker ways to kill myself. Besides the booze. A far-off foghorn is warning ships away from the cliffs. It's a sad sound, long and low. I can taste on my teeth what I drank all night. Penny is asleep on her back on the mattress next to me. She's snoring and her store-bought tits rise and fall, and her breath fills the room. It's not a bad smell; she smokes clove cigarettes, chews cinnamon-flavor gum. Her face is still pretty. The window that overlooks Green Street is open and there's a chill and I put the white sheet over her white legs. I want to protect her, keep her safe and warm. She moves a little and turns onto her side, facing away from me, and I close my eyes.

Other drunks, downstairs at Gino and Carlo, are playing pool and laughing and I can hear them, smell pizza at Golden Boy's as well as our eager but empty sex from earlier. I get out of bed. Feel around the floor for my pants and shirt and put them on. Step into my shoes. I can make last call, if Frankie Junior is not pissed at me. Penny will be afraid if she wakes up alone, because she needs to refill her prescription, but that simply isn't something I can worry about anymore. I need to find my own balance again.

Frankie Junior sees me and shakes his head slowly but nonetheless gets down the dusty bottle of Old Crow. Pours a stiff one over dirty ice cubes. Sets it in front of me. He doesn't say a word and he doesn't have to and neither do I because his dad and me, we go way back. A fruit fly lands on the lip of my glass. The Giants are on the television and Barry Bonds pops one into McCovey Cove. I put the drink where it belongs and my throat warms. Tom Linehan rubs my shoulders like a cornerman at a professional bout. When I see my face in the mirror, I barely recognize it—it isn't even me anymore. Pete Crudo is belting out Sinatra tunes. He used to have a gig in Vegas. He keeps a condo in Boca and refers to Sammy Davis as *the muthafucka of muthafuckas.* He sits next to me and buys me drinks until I'm thirsty again. He sees himself as a father figure. Then Tony Machi shows up with a flashlight and a plastic Safeway bag heavy with snails he found on the trail to Coit Tower. After keeping them in a cardboard box for a week he'll roll them in cornmeal and brown them in sweet butter. He tells me the recipe twice—he says everything twice. This town is full of characters and I am the king of the misfits.

Then there's a problem near the bathroom and Frankie Senior wants me to take care of it because that's what I do. And he'll give me a free refill for my efforts. He tells me some college kid punched a hole in the sheetrock after he scratched on the eight ball. The dude is built like a linebacker. I place a cocktail napkin over my glass and get up and head to the back. The college boy tries to defend himself but it's no use since he hesitates and that is the worst mistake you can make against a guy like me. Penny says I have a mean streak a mile wide and maybe she's right about that. I take him into the alley and hit him until he stops moving, but I don't feel mean about it. I don't feel anything at all.

There's a drizzle and the faded yellow curb is chipped and

slick and I sit on it and roll a fat one to catch my breath. My lungs burn in that good way. A clean-cut young couple leaving the new bistro is looking sideways at the mess I have made. I smile and wave, blow smoke rings. It must be a scene. That wouldn't be a bad way to go—face down in the street. But the kid isn't dead, he just needs some stitches and to give his ribs a rest. Fog rounds the corner like a gang of hooligan ghosts and a rat slips up from the sewer looking for food. I haven't had a meal in four days. Penny cooks but I don't eat in hopes that I'll simply disappear. A skinny sapling with tiny red flowers pushes up from a crack in the sidewalk.

Frankie Junior mops the floor with poison while Frankie Senior counts the cash. It was a profitable night. He gives me a little for my trouble and puts some aside to get the wall patched tomorrow. I finish my drink and say goodnight. Frankie Senior kisses my cheeks European style, bolts the door behind me.

My key sticks in the lock to the apartment as usual. Penny is squatting in a corner of the room, pulling her knees up against her chest. So, she woke up and got scared and now I feel like shit about it. I settle in next to her and put my arm around her and I tell her that everything is all right. I hold tight and rock back and forth. It's all right, baby, I say.

After a while she believes me and stops shivering and puts her head on my shoulder. Her heart flutters like butterfly wings. It's raining outside and coming sideways through the open window. I feel it on my face and neck and knuckles that are bleeding. Then she gets up and burns incense while I use my library card to chop up some gack on the glass-top coffee table. She partakes and then does her clumsy version of a striptease. More for her than for me at this point; she needs to feel beautiful and desired. I clap my hands. She smiles, kneels naked in front of me, and puts her face in my lap. I stare at her flaking scalp, the dark roots of her bleached hair. She cries softly as she unzips me. Candles on the ledge, a siren in Chinatown. She puts me in her mouth. I close my eyes.

***

My brother the Queer rubs his eyes with his thumbs when mom tells us that he has a different father. It isn't so much the news as the cocaine he's just hoovered up his nose. My other brother, Jake, calls my mother a whore. He's the oldest, retired Navy. We're sitting in the kitchen, wrapping up a family meeting. I'm drinking all the cooking sherry and everything else in sight. Earlier in the week we learned that a bridge worker on the Golden Gate found Dad's wallet on the handrail, and so he alerted the authorities. They checked the tides and the current and found him washed up on Baker Beach a couple days later—the saltwater had done a number on him. I hadn't seen the old man in years and don't even recall what our rift was over. It was always something with him and me. And, truth be told, I always figured him for a jumper.

It's a good thing Dad is dead, Jake says.

He's referring, of course, to my mother's news flash regarding her ancient act of infidelity.

He makes a sign of the cross, ends at his lips.

But on the other hand, this does explain a lot, he says.

I try to respond but it seems that I no longer have the capacity for language.

Mom won't say who the Queer's father is. She says it's none of our goddamn business. I'm in no position to judge, especially since Penny gave me the boot again and I'm living in a broke-down RV in my mother's one-car garage—the same RV we used to take on road trips to Yosemite back when we were pretending to be a normal family.

It's just a temporary arrangement. I don't expect to live much longer.

Penny doesn't need me anymore because her goofball shrink can get her better drugs. I always knew it was just a matter of time with her, but that doesn't lessen the sting. She put all my things in a trash bag on the stoop with a note.

But we've been through this routine before.

My mother is playing a Bing Crosby album that skips when Jake and the Queer start throwing hands over the estate—Dad wasn't rich by any definition but there's property up north and a retirement fund. She tries to break them up with her metal cane and falls. Just like old times, I manage to say. She rolls over and gets stuck like a turtle under the card table. The boys keep slugging, ignoring her hopeless flailing. It is a sight. So fucking funny and pathetic and sad that I laugh. Eventually I help her up and then Jake puts the Queer through the kitchen window. Mom grabs her chest. Neighbors call the cops in Spanish. Officer Lopez radios an ambulance for the Queer's concussion and my mother's bad ticker. Then they ride together to San Francisco General, where they'll stay twenty-four hours for observation. Alabama Street to Cesar Chavez to Portrero Avenue. Mission District cops are Latino-tough, and Jake gets pepper-sprayed and tasered and hogtied and he'll spend the night at 850 Bryant. He's a real fighter, that one. I'll pick him up in the morning, but it's nice to have the house to myself for a change. I try to sleep in my mother's bed but it smells like the worst parts of her.

***

Two weeks later I smoke one of Penny's skinny cigarettes in the dark alley between Jesus Loves You and Adult Video. We're back together again, back on that fucking merry-go-round. It's past midnight. I hear what sounds like a cat dying about halfway down, where a fence has been erected, and I go closer to investigate. The poor stray took a busted chain link right through the eyeball. Maybe she got chased by a dog or a raccoon or maybe she'd been hunting a rat. She's stuck and really thrashing about, hissing at me like I put her there, looking at me with that one crazy angry eye spinning around in its socket. I let her get used to me for a minute and then I move behind and try to calm her with my voice. I put both hands around her ribs and count, one, two, three, and in one smooth motion slide her off clean, letting her go over my hip. Then the cat is gone so fast it's like she was never even there. A few scratches on my arm but not bad.

They say cats get nine lives and I wonder if that's a blessing or a curse.

Then Penny is comatose, which is normal for a Sunday. She danced Saturday at The Hungry I until two in the morning and then pulled a private party afterward. I know all about those private parties, but it's good money, especially considering that her best years are far behind her. Last rainy season she told me that young girls with big tits were making the serious dough, and she'd heard about a doctor in Redwood City; the Vietnamese woman who does her nails said he was the best and cheapest in Northern California. So, I gave her all the money I'd just won on a fast horse at Bay Meadows. She had the procedure done the following month.

She's snoring now. I wash the cat off my hands and make a nightcap of Southern Comfort and warm milk and watch Penny sleep from a metal folding chair. Her hair is wet, water staining the pillow, because she likes to shower after being groped by strangers all night long. I can't even imagine what that is like.

There is an empty bottle of pills on the floor alongside a glass that is also empty except for a few melting ice cubes. She's wearing one of my old wife-beaters and a pair of cotton shorts. I wonder what she's dreaming. I hope it's about having nice things. I hope I'm not in it. She's a good and decent girl, and she deserves more than I can ever give her.

***

Then they stick my father in the ground in Colma and I'm wearing a monkey suit borrowed from my old friend Mike Shannon. There are nip bottles in the back of the limo and when empty they make music in my coat pocket. I'm riding with my mother and her friend Florence and my brothers. I close my eyes and wake up at Tony Nick's and the Giants have lost to the fucking Dodgers. A guy in an LA t-shirt says something smart to me and I put him on the floor and crouch over him and rain my fists on the parts he leaves unprotected. I'm not angry, there's no emotion, it's just a thing I do. The violence allows me to focus, to slow down the world so I can function in it. Everybody wants me to stop but there's no stopping me now. Tom Petty is on the juke singing *stop dragging my heart around.* Somebody grabs the old rotary phone to call for help. Fog from outside slips in the front door slow. A wood chair breaks and a door comes off its hinges and more fresh air wafts in off the bay. Broken glass. A flawless white tooth is lodged in the flat middle knuckle of my right hand. With my left, I have somebody by the ankle.

It takes four rookie cops to subdue me in the middle of Green Street while Sergeant O'Barry directs traffic around us and laughs and smokes a cheap cigar and tells them to cut off my circulation with the plastic straps they often use now instead of metal handcuffs. He's been arresting me for years. I curse his mother and cat-hiss whiskey at him. He uses his boots on my face until one eye swells shut and then he eats a slice of pepperoni-and-mushroom from next door while his boys tuck in their crisp shirts and clean up with napkins; fast learners. O'Barry's chin is shiny with cheese drippings. Then they shove me in the back of his wagon and at North Station use a hose on me that splotches my skin red. They give me a jumper that is too small, and I stand freezing in a corner of the cell. Then Sergeant O'Barry sticks his head in and says, Sorry about your pop. He knew my father from their days coaching for the Catholic Youth Organization.

***

My head hurts and I wake up in a soft bed and look at the sun outside. My eyes water so I pull the curtain closed. I don't remember being released but my memory isn't what it used to be. There's a radio playing softly from the bathroom and somebody is banging a hammer in perfect rhythm next door. I get my bearings: I'm in Lorraine's studio on Market Street. She lets me crash here sometimes. Mornings she waits tables at a twelve-seat café on California and Polk. I look at the clock on the wall over the stove; her shift has already started. The small kitchen smells like oatmeal. There is a bowl that she has prepared for me on the counter and I get a spoon and scoop it all into the trash—the brown mush and the raisins and the walnuts. The thought of eating makes my stomach turn. I sit on a chair and smoke a cigarette and another. Then I stand up and get sick in the sink. The hammer next door. I count my ribs in the shower and lead pipes complain and steam rises to the ceiling.

Lorraine shakes me awake by the shoulders. I open my eyes. She's wearing a big t-shirt that goes down to her knees. It's old and yellow and advertises Hamburger Mary's. I sit up and rub my face with my hands and she touches the top of my head. We stay like that for a while. The day is almost gone and I have the shakes. She smiles. Jesus Christ. Her smile always fills me with something new.

Boy, you going to kill yourself.

Shit, girl.

Well, don't do it here then.

All right.

I get up and she puts her arms around me and gives me a squeeze. I can smell the lotion she uses to keep her skin as smooth as polished wood. She's a beautiful girl. I let her hug me for a while and then I don't, and she shakes her head and avoids my eyes. I find my clothes and get dressed and she goes about her business—putting some groceries in the refrigerator, hanging up the wet towel I left on the floor near the bathtub, checking her answering machine. There's a nasty message from a credit card company. She owes them a bit of money it seems. I owe her more than money so when she's not looking, I leave the remains of the cash that Frankie Senior gave me next to the lamp on the end table. With any luck that will hold her over. I'm out of cigarettes too.

See you, I say.

You don't have to go.

Yeah, I do.

I can fix us a drink.

I shake my head. I'm tempted but I need to be out on the street for a while. That's part of my sickness too: uncomfortable indoors, near people, uncomfortable in my own skin. I turn to the door and she follows me. I undo the deadbolt and open it, take a step so that I'm straddling the threshold. She puts a hand on my shoulder and I stop.

Call me later, she says.

All right.

I probably won't call her later. I won't even remember that we had this conversation. But I don't say that. I don't say anything else and she shuts the door. I hear the lock go into place and I dig my fists into my pockets to steady them. It's five flights down and the elevator is busted. The stairwell smells like piss. A crackhead is curled up at the bottom and I step over him. I open the door and the sky is bright and pigeons scatter into the street and shit on the pavement. A dented taxicab jumps the curb and almost runs me down and then rights itself and disappears. I don't even flinch. That could've been it right there. The end of the line. Then John P. the bartender is complaining about washing dishes. It's Mario's on Grant and Green. It's mostly a bar but they serve paninis and salads and soft potatoes fried in recycled olive oil. I used to play ball with John when we were kids. He was a hell of an athlete. You wouldn't know it to look at him now. I can hardly remember what I was like back then.

It's just crap is what I'm saying, he says.

He keeps on about the dishes and I tune him out as best I can. Like I give two shits. I drink until I feel normal again. John wants Mario to hire some Mexicans, but the old man is too cheap, and he admits it. And besides, he thinks they'll rob him blind. He's racist against non-Italians. He hates some Italians too but mostly he reserves it for the others. I nod my head as long as John keeps pouring. There is some of that rap crap playing on the juke in the corner. I'm going to smash it to pieces. I close my eyes and try to get my mind straight. Then I'm sitting on a bench in Washington Square. A tall tree casts a long shadow on a faded brick wall. The smell of fresh-baked focaccia. Children running down the steps of St. Paul's. A line around the block for Mama's. Cars and graffiti-scrawled busses and messengers on beat-up bikes. And fumes from all of it.

Kevin Moretti stops his white pickup on Columbus and taps the horn. He waves me over. He has work for me if I need some scratch. He runs a paint crew. Mostly residential. I get in and we're going to a house in the Sunset District. It's an interior job. He'll give me twenty bucks an hour. We take Kearny to California to Presidio. After the park it turns into Nineteenth Avenue and we follow that to Taraval Street. There is fog and I get a chill and we double-park and get out for coffees at Tennessee Grill. It's mostly Asians in this part of town now. Then Kevin drops me off and gives me the keys and the house is empty except for buckets and brushes and heavy sheets to protect the hardwood floors, and I paint the kitchen eggshell and the dining room a shade of purple and the hallway some sort of tan color. The walls were already prepped, which is perfect. It's a good day's work. The backyard is overgrown with weeds and orange wildflowers that cling to a green vine. I sit on a stump and smoke a cigarette from the pack Kevin gave me as part of an advance. I hear the L train sliding down the hill on its copper-colored rails toward Ocean Beach, where whales go to die sometimes. The birds get to them and the dogs and the flies do too, and the stink of it carries for miles and miles.

Kevin comes back with a sixer of tall boys. He tells me about his golf game. He has a time share in Palm Springs. He did time at Lompoc and his neck displays the crude ink to prove it. We smoke cigarettes and drink beer and then we lock up the house and his truck and walk to the Dragon Lounge. It used to be Fahey's. Kevin runs a tab and we go into the shitter a couple times for a toot. Then the place fills up with off-duty five-oh from Taraval Station and some of them are all right with me and others are not. Kevin gets nervous. The Giants are on the television. Santiago hits a dinger. The girl behind the bar is half Chinese and wearing a short skirt and a too-small tank top and silver earrings that dangle. The young cops are all over her and I don't blame them for trying.

***

Then Penny won't come to the door. My old key doesn't work. I don't know what I'm doing anymore. Why I'm bothering. But I do know there's a man in the flat with her and she knows that I will mess him up bad. She's going to ring the police. I don't care about that. I call her a whore even though I know it's not true, not the way I mean it. She begs me to leave and she's crying. It seems she has forgotten how she used to need me, and I say as much. How soon we forget and all that nonsense. I just want to talk—that's what I say, and it was true at first but now I want to fuck her also. Funny how that works. Whoever is in there with her isn't making a peep, so I probably know him from the neighborhood. Or he knows me and what I'm likely to do when I see him. Then my brother the Queer comes to get me. Penny reached him at our mother's house. His eyes are big. He's scared of me. Everybody is scared of me when I get like this.

Come on, he says. Let's go.

Fucking whore.

Come on.

He takes my arm and I let him because he's my brother and he is soft.

You're lucky she didn't call the cops, he says.

I tell him that he's the lucky one. He looks at me.

That I don't fuck you up, I say.

Oh, that. I thought you meant lucky I have you as a role model.

Yeah that too, I say, trying not to smile.

But I laugh and he does too. The Queer can always make me laugh. Even when we were coming up, he always had that ability. He tells me that Jake is still pissed about the other night. Mostly at our mother but also at him. I tell him not to worry about it. Jake will stay away for a few weeks, maybe go shoot some ducks at his camp near Russian River, and then he'll forgive and forget. The guy can't hold a grudge. It isn't in his chemistry. The Queer agrees and feels better now—except for the bruised skull Jake gave him Sunday. He's supposed to meet a guy at Kimo's. We take a cab to Pine Street and I pay for it. It's all pole smokers in the club but I don't care about that. My brother orders a drink that is some kind of apple-flavored martini. I buy a couple rounds for him and his buddy named Adolfo, who seems like good people, which puts me at ease; the Queer deserves to be happy. Then the trolley comes shoving down California lugging tourists to the financial district. I smell Greek pizza and Swan's oysters and the flower shop.

***

John P. tells me Mike Shannon is banging Penny behind my back. I don't say anything. Apparently, it's been going on for months and I'm the last to know. My head starts to hurt. I look around for somebody to hit but the joint is empty. He pours me a shot of Jack Daniels. The front of his shirt is dry because Mario finally hired a Mexican. Then I soak the suit I borrowed from Mike in gasoline and burn it on the sidewalk. Mrs. DeMartini yells from her second story sublet that she's going to call the fire marshal. Then Lorraine invites me to dinner. She slow-cooked a corned beef for her godson's baptism and has leftovers. Garlic mashed potatoes. Cherry-tomato salad with goat cheese. She puts it on a plate for me. I can't stand the thought of eating. I look at it for a few minutes and she sits there watching me. Then I tell her about Penny. At first, she looks dejected, moves her chair closer to mine, takes my hands in hers and cries. Runs her fingers along my narrow wrists, blue-rope veins. She smiles. Jesus. There it is again. I almost smile too.

You're wasting away, she says. A fucking skeleton.

Right.

Well, now it's just you and me then.

She's glad Penny's out of the picture, even though she'd never admit it. She wants to mend me. She likes projects. Lorraine gets up and lets me take her pants off. Then I'm standing behind her and she puts me deep inside and we bump against each other like that for a while. That's how I fix things, make them right at least for the time being. Besides the various substances and the fights, that's the only way I know how. She wants me to finish but I can't anymore, and she gets upset and cries and so we keep trying until we're too tired. Finishing isn't critical to me—it's the trying. Once I'm there it's always disappointing because I end up so empty and alone.

She falls asleep and I go into the bathroom until my hands are sticky with the mess I make. I clean up. Then the meal is still on the table and I stab a piece of cold meat with a thin layer of fat on the edge and take a bite. Chewing is unfamiliar and I go slow, but the food is fine, and I only gag a little. I use a stale heel of buttered sourdough to soak up the last of the gravy. Then the sun comes up over rooftops and among white clouds, and a bony brown bird sits on a buzzing telephone wire. Startled, it flaps madly and disappears from sight but returns within seconds. There are others too, gray with yellow eyes and bigger wings, but this one stands out in its persistence. I watch it forever. Then my head hurts and I get in bed and rest it against Lorraine's chest. She wakes up and whispers bullshit in my ear until I nearly believe it and I slowly close my eyes.

blister

blue Chevy pickup &
we whispered waiting

windshield rain & dead mosquitos
his wife serving drinks

he kissed me French &
took my photo on the roof deck
when
the San Francisco Bay chopped lonely to taste
our lips

Fat Jack's meatloaf & mashed potatoes
beatdown backstreets & budweiser faggots
Jim Beam chess champion laughing
ha

drugstore lambskin sixpack &
his Mastercard gold motel
room
sandy sheets & he cried beautiful &
in my ear he hum tongued a song
moved my arm to free his hair

I heard him on the toilet &
he rolled over me
his

hand on my stomach & face on my tit
he thought I was dreaming
& maybe I was

east wind made us walk &
        towed our voices through traffic

light house   that dirty fucking eye
watching   &
white boy's outer bar loud & louder &
Violent Femmes scream blister in the sun

city redneck wanted nice but got me
so he danced alone &
the bad moon offered bully boxes
~ eskimo

LAVA RATS

They call him Salt because of his hair and he loves the ocean. Joey meets him and the other Lava Rats in the dunes where Taraval Street pours into the Pacific. Salt carries his long board against his hip and barks out a greeting when he sees Joey. Jeff and Greenie and Bean Counter are there too. It's early and Salt puts on his second skin. The water is rough and cold, and they paddle out until Salt holds up his hand and then everybody waits. He lets Joey go first and he catches a pretty good wave. The others follow on inconsistent swells and with varying degrees of success. Then Joey watches Salt and he's so smooth as usual on a real beauty. The guy is a natural born water man.

Later the sun is punching fat holes in nimbus clouds and Salt's girlfriend brings his dog and some tuna sandwiches and beers for everybody. Joey plays with the dog named Jigs. They wrestle in the sand. Joggers jog and fathers skip rocks for sons.

Salt's girlfriend cleans up after everybody and takes the dog home. She kisses Salt goodbye on the forehead and he's in the middle of a story, so he ignores her. He's holding court and that is what he does. She's wearing Capri pants that are low cut and fit her curves just right and a little swatch of her soft cotton panties is showing in the back at the belt line. Joey breathes in to get a whiff of her and he can't help but look and his mind takes off running. Fuck me, he thinks. Salt's girl notices and walks away swinging those hips extra like a dinner bell and the dog flops alongside her. Joey's shoulders are tired and his head hurts, so he begs off and watches the rest of them go. He closes his eyes.

Then some fucking Barney drops in on Bean Counter and Salt chases him down. It's hard to tell what all goes on out there but before you know it the guy is surrounded and underwater and when he comes to shore, he has taken a good beating. He throws up and bleeds a little where he'll need stitches. He crouches for a few minutes trying to gather himself because it looks like he has sucked up a good amount of water. He doesn't notice but Joey watches a fist-size crab digging itself into the mud and waiting to taxi back out to sea. It's slow but it entrenches itself so that only its hard shell is showing just a little. It feels protected. Then Salt and Jeff come ashore and finish what they'd started until the Barney is just lying there. Somebody must've seen the incident and called the cops or at least alerted the lifeguards on patrol in their white and red pickup truck.

There's been talk of installing cameras to record the violent outbursts that are viewed by locals as a necessary part of this unique sub-culture but have been increasing with the influx of unskilled surfers. Fucking hipsters and technology workers and whatnot. Joey grabs the guy's plank and they leave. Salt wants to surf Fort Point now. Fuck this fucking faggot-ass beach, he says. Bean Counter makes sure the guy is breathing. Greenie is last and sees the crab and steps on it, Joey hears the crushing sound.

marooned

live my life
selfless
die my death
selfish

never swim again
the Barbary
Coast &
the
marooned

inside the empty spoon

~ eskimo

THE WHEELS ARE COMING OFF

I was getting a tan in Washington Square. One-Legged Johnny fought in Vietnam and stepped on a land mine. He was still pissed about it. He came by with Big Al Ma. Big Al worked in the pantry of the President Roosevelt ship for almost thirty years. At thirty years he could retire with his pension. One month shy they fired him for being a drunk.

But he'd been a drunk for that entire stretch.

So, you might say the timing was suspicious.

One-Legged Johnny and Al were broke. They didn't ask me for anything. They never did. I'd just won money on Tiger Slew at Bay Meadows. It was a hunch. I sent Big Al to the corner for a twelve-pack of Pabst. We drank it in the sun. All the cops knew us, but this rookie walked up. He said we couldn't drink in the park. I apologized, and One-Legged Johnny and I dumped our beers. Big Al Ma kept drinking. And the rookie kept talking and finally he grabbed the beer away from him and Big Al pulled a steak knife out of his coat. I don't know where he got it or what he thought he was going to do with it.

It happened so fast.

Big Al was only about four-and-a-half feet tall and weighed maybe a hundred pounds soaking wet. He was under arrest with a knee on his spine before you knew it.

One-Legged Johnny couldn't stop laughing.

We hit Golden Boy for a slice of pepperoni. Gino and Carlo had the usual crowd. It was Saturday afternoon. Pierre was in there smiling through his one tooth. I once saw him carry a refrigerator up five flights of stairs. I bought him a shot of Old Crow. He stunk to high heaven. The Iranian was in there bothering people. I told Brent behind the bar that the Iranian had to go but Brent said he was still breaking him in. Brent liked projects. He liked to say that I was one of his projects and look how I turned out. It was true. I used to be in worse shape. I raised my glass to him. The Giants were on the television. Santiago hit a two-run dinger.

Brown Sugar saw me standing by the bathroom. I was making sure One-Legged Johnny got out of there okay. She put her quarters down for a game of pool. She told me she was available if I wanted to come by her place later. She had a clean little apartment in a dirty building on Market Street. She was a decent girl. She stripped at a joint on Larkin where stripping wasn't the only thing she did. It was good money and I sure wasn't in a position to judge anybody. I told her I probably wouldn't be able to walk that far. She told me to take a cab. One part of me wanted to go and a bigger part of me did not. One-Legged Johnny fell against the door so I couldn't even get to him. He pissed all over himself. The Iranian had some smart things to say to us, so I socked him in the lip. I used to get paid to hit people as hard as I hit him. Brown Sugar got out of the way. I told Brent behind the bar that I was sorry, and we left so he wouldn't have to ask us to leave.

***

I used to have a wife. She taught school. She said she divorced me because of my drinking and that was before I really started drinking. That sucked everything out of me for years. She was a local girl too and every now and then I hear things about her and I'm glad she is doing better. She has a nice house in the

Bernal Heights and a family and all the things I could never give to her. I think she married an investment guy from back east somewhere, maybe Connecticut. For a while I called her a two-timing whore but that was never the case. Now even when one of my brothers eggs me on just for kicks, I can't think of a bad thing to say about her. She is perfect in memory.

***

One-Legged Johnny didn't want to go to La Rocca's. That is what he would do. He would hit the wall. So, I bought him a turkey sandwich and some gnocchi and a half pint of Jim Beam. I gave him half a pack of smokes. I left him on a bench in the shade. Doug was working and he had my drink poured before I sat down. Some fat fucking punk from the Marina I used to knock the shit out of was sizing me up. In the old days, I would've started in on him right away, but I let it go. I let everything go now. Older and wiser. All that nonsense. The Giants lost to the Braves. There was basketball on too. When Doug's shift ended then Erin with her curly blond hair took over. I sang pop songs to her and she rolled her eyes at me. She was young and she had a couple young boyfriends hanging out at the end of the bar keeping tabs on me. Then they helped her push me out the door at closing time but weren't as rough as they could've been—they didn't know me from Adam, and I wouldn't have blamed them for trying.

I sat in the park for a while. A few kids from Alice Griffith rolled some tech bro who had veered off course. I recognized them from Salesian. It was pretty harmless. He was all right. I helped him up and his nose was busted and needed some attention. I told him to get it looked at. He pushed me away and called me an old drunk. I hailed a cab and told the driver to bring me to Market and Sixth. I couldn't remember her exact address. If he dropped me there, I could find it. Brown Sugar buzzed me up. She was burning incense. She told me she won four or five games of pool and the Iranian was talking shit the whole time. That fucking guy. She went to mix a couple drinks but then she could tell that I'd had it. Her bed was soft. I didn't want to talk anymore because my head hurt. I got these headaches. She undressed me. Her skin was smooth in most places. She put a rubber on me and used some jelly on herself to save me the trouble. Then she did all the work, but it was a good long time until she was able to finish. She was a professional and took pride in what she could do but I was too numb to really feel anything. I was happy to help her fall asleep. And the visuals of all we had just done would help me later when I was alone.

***

When I woke up, she was gone and there was a fat black cockroach inches from my face on the pillow. I checked my roll of cash and it was a bit smaller but that was an understanding we had. I picked up Big Al Ma at North Station. He needed a drink in the worst way. He told me that jail wasn't bad. They gave him some food that tasted like a peanut butter sandwich and an old blanket that smelled like mildew. They let him call his sister, but his brother-in-law answered and wouldn't put him through. They had disowned him years ago. They used to have a sweet little studio in the garage for him. He had told me this story a million times, but I let him continue because I didn't have the energy to stop him. He was crying. I put my arm around him and we stood like that.

He came from Hong Kong in 1961. He traveled the world on the President Roosevelt. After he got fucked out of his pension, he didn't know what to do. He moved in with his sister's family and drank whatever he could get his hands on. It was bad for the children, so his brother-in-law told him to leave. They kept his savings and his monthly social security checks and gave him an allowance. It was enough to pay for a hotel room and meals but that was about it, so he was always asking for more. Eventually they got tired of him bothering them, so they opened an account at Wells Fargo and let him do what he wanted. He told me that was a great day. He used the word freedom. But you can't give a drunk unfettered access to funds like that because we'll piss it all away in no time, which is what he did. He looked up at me and his eyes were dried out and blank. Big Al shuddered and I held onto him tight so he wouldn't blow away in the wind.

dreams

father
with his
dick on fire

sister twisted
on a tree

drunken mother
drinks her comfort
almond eyes obscene

tearless
torment &
high desire

I shed
these skins from me

brilliance blackened
love's fate fastened
he needs someone who
dreams
~ eskimo

WAITING FOR THE WHISTLE

Sunny but cold and the wind works like a sandblaster. Trash cans upended and Doggie Diner wrappers and *Bay Guardians* get caught in a mini tornado on the sidewalk in front of Kezar Stadium. Inside are guys with names like Snake and Bucky and IQ. Children swarm the court in between quarters. Bing Dionida is doing color commentary and making smartass comments over a microphone from the scorer's table. Barry Stiles is sitting in the bleachers with his back against the concrete wall, drinking a forty. He used to ball with some of these cats down at the Cage, the Panhandle and even Russian Hill.

Tommy eats a slice of pepperoni and cheese from North Beach Pizza across the street, really getting into it, there is cheese in his new beard and his chin is oily. Barry tells him to slow down. Slow down, you fat fuck, he says. You're making me sick.

Tommy laughs it off like everything else.

Kezar isn't too packed because there aren't any pros there tonight. Local boys with jobs. A few scouts taking notes. One high school-age terror from Oakland named Raeshon Benton— and a half-dozen guys from D1 programs. Hook Mitchell never even graduated from anywhere, but he has major dumb-dumbs and is a local legend. Barry watched him dunk over a Volkswagen Bug in Golden Gate Park several years ago. It was some kind of competition and of course he won with that move. He doesn't even really look like a basketball player. He's compact and explosive rather than long and lean and graceful. When he was coming up people used to underestimate him but that was before he had made a name for himself, had established himself as a force. And, of course, that was way before he had ruined his future in hoops by robbing a video store at gunpoint.

Wilson Stephens elevates and drops two points on Ali Thomas' head, but the youngster takes it pretty well and the crowd shows its appreciation. Barry used to hoop with Thomas at Presidio, a decent YMCA run on Saturday mornings. Tommy claps his hands together. Barry finishes his beer. Nick the Cop is working the crowd and he gives Barry a look when he sees the brown paper bag in his lap. Barry uses exaggerated hand signals and facial gestures to indicate he's done drinking, nothing to worry about, no need to come over and bust his chops. Nick shakes his head, disappointed, but also distracted by a rowdy group of bangers from Visitacion Valley making noise in the corner.

After the game Barry crosses the street with Tommy to Kezar Pub. They eat shepherd's pie. It's a clear, crisp night and people milling about outside, smoking, talking shit. At a bar on Clement Street, Barry and Tommy get to rapping with some gal, trying to get her friend named Linda to join them but there's some kind of boyfriend trouble. The boyfriend looks like a tweaker and Barry says as much. They're arguing in the street and the boyfriend tosses his lit cigarette at Linda. Apparently, he likes the junk and he's been freeloading for more than a year and his girlfriend has finally had enough. He looks undernourished and with those skinny heroin muscles you often see inside and other places. Barry offers to help with the current situation, but the girl just laughs because she thinks he's joking, and he guesses she and Linda just want to let things work themselves out. That's the way some people are, but he doesn't understand that level of passivity.

He likes to take the bull by the horns.

That's his personal motto.

A pal of Tommy's shows up later. He's from the old country and Tommy says he's straight-up IRA. Barry can't understand a word he says with that fucking accent and he gives him a bad feeling, so he pulls a disappearing act. Houdini. Trap fucking door. It's getting late by now. He sees a good-looking college girl in the window of a bookstore, so he goes inside and stalks her up and down the aisles until she goes for help and he laughs. The geek at the register is in way over his head so Barry gives him a break. He's just being silly because she's not his type and he leaves without a problem. There's a café across the street and a smartass teenager with three rings in her nose makes a lousy cup of cocoa and he reads as much of the *SF Weekly* as he can concentrate on. He looks for a cab but hears loud music, so he walks into this bar. It's hopping mad in there.

He's the tallest person in the joint and he can tell they're fresh-off-the-boat. The men are older and wearing nice suits and the women are younger and have great fake tits. Barry gets to thinking about Shrimp Boy and the Hop Sing Crew of the Chinese crime syndicate, which has been getting a lot of press lately. Everybody looks at him standing there and the music did seem to stop for a few beats soon as he walked in the door. Might as well shine a spotlight on me, he thinks. He nudges his way to the bar to get a drink and the hot bartender in Daisy Duke cut-offs doesn't speak English so she gets nervous and goes away and is soon replaced by this dude in a too-small shirt with gym-induced, fake-ass muscles popping out everywhere. Barry asks what kind of beer on tap and dude goes through a laundry list and Barry orders a Tsingtao and dude tries to charge him eight dollars for a glass. Barry makes a face like to say *what the fuck* and the bartender says it isn't a public bar. It's a private party, he says in his busted English.

Barry tells him he just wants a goddamn beer, but the prick isn't going to budge on price. So, next best thing, Barry scrambles over the maplewood counter and crushes the bartender's Adam's apple between his thumb and bent finger and all those little fuckers start crowding him back there and he's seen too many movies to not know how this is going to end up. They'll find pieces of him in the bay. He decides to call it a night. Raps knuckles against a few hard skulls and disappears out the door and into the fog.

***

The sunset is stacked clouds like alternating layers of ice cream; strawberry and vanilla and blue. A stray dog barks and ropey weeds crack the sidewalk. There's a white sailboat out there too. Barry smokes a cigarette and strokes the stray dog's belly and the Fungs are barbecuing salmon steaks from the Chinese Super on Mission Street, the one next door to Patio Español. Then Barry watches the fog snuff out the stars one at a time and then the lunatic moon is gone too. The dog scratches at a flea and barks and takes off running.

There is a storm coming down the coast from Canada. People are talking about El Niño. There's a knock on the door but Barry isn't expecting anybody. He puts on pants and pokes his head out. It's Trey Johnson, just finished his paper route. He played hoops for the Dons back in the glory days, just before the program got suspended, then tried out for the Boston Celtics a couple times. Played in Israel and the Philippines. Chased the dream until his body wouldn't let him anymore. He sees Barry for a bump now and again.

Can you believe it, Trey says.

Barry shakes his head.

A grown-ass man delivering newspapers, Trey says.

Barry laughs. Folks always assume Trey got his degree from USF, but nobody ever asks and it's certainly clear that he hasn't benefited from any academics. It's a shame because he has four children to feed. His wife works at juvenile hall as a counselor. Trey stands in the doorway and Barry cracks him a can of beer. He's on a list to get a job with the water department in Marin. His knees are shot so he isn't even playing pickup anymore, but they call him a legend down at Kezar during pro-am season. He pays Barry some of the money he owes even though Barry isn't asking for it. Tells him hold onto the cash until he gets a steady gig, but Trey doesn't want it hanging over his head. He's a good dude like that. He doesn't hardly fit in Barry's flat with his big-ass frame, so they go outside to sit on the stoop and drink beer and shoot the shit a while.

Trey bitches about job prospects.

Should of never even gone to school, he says.

Barry nods his head.

Straight to the fucking pros, Trey says.

No shit. Like Kobe.

But nobody was doing that back then.

Ain't that some shit.

Now I'm just waiting for the whistle.

Trey's old Jap car is double-parked and too small for a big man and stuffed with the newspapers that he's supposed to have delivered. The engine is running. Barry tells him how Heavy D and Jandro have a regular thing at the Presidio Y on Saturday mornings and he should go down sometime for a game or two just for the hell of it. See some familiar faces. Trey says he will, but Barry knows it's a load of shit. Tough enough for him to walk twenty feet due to all the damn knee operations and vertebrae fusions.

After a half hour or so Trey unfolds himself and pushes his fist against Barry's and manages to contort into his little Celica that looks like it has skin cancer. Barry smokes a joint and Trey honks the horn and then the transplant across the street looks up at Barry and waves. Barry can't stand that motherfucker but he's coming over for a chat now. Hey buddy, what's it doing, Transplant says. Barry raps with him for about as long as he can stand it, which is only a matter of minutes. Then the guy finally asks Barry if he can talk to him about Kenny yelling at all hours of the night. He asks if Barry can tell Kenny not to curse out the window at his children when they're walking home from school. Asks Barry if he can get his older brother who's disabled to stop sleeping in his yard under the lemon tree. When he's done asking, Barry just looks at him. Tells him his brother checked himself into Laguna Honda last Thursday, so he won't be sleeping under the lemon tree for a while. And if you don't like it here you can always go back where you came from, Barry says. They're eyeball-to-eyeball now and Barry blows smoke in his face until Transplant coughs. He stops coughing and walks away mumbling under his breath about karma is a bitch. Barry flicks the roach at his head, calls him a useless prick.

***

Three young skateboarders blast down the hill toward Ocean Beach and the purple sunset that awaits them. A fourth boy is following the trio in a minivan just about covered in stickers advertising Mr. Zog's Sex Wax, *Thrasher Magazine* and Billabong, and he's got his hand out the window, holding a small video camera to film his friends' dusk descent. Barry lights a Marlboro with his Zippo and watches them go by and the kid driving the van looks over at him and smiles. He tilts his chin and points his cigarette at the bushy haired little bastard and blows smoke through his nostrils like that old charging bull.

shoot

you said

look at me

& he did &

with our orange
thoughts

we laughed

at
the sound
of the gun

& the old Chinese lady

screamed &
dropped her plastic Safeway bag in the street

~ eskimo

BEFORE I WRECK EVERYTHING ELSE

The blonde waitress from the café tosses her cigarette into the street. She's wearing a tight black tube top that shows off her midriff. Smoke comes from her mouth like from the exhaust pipe of an old American car. Just then an old Buick Regal stops at the intersection of Taraval Street and Twenty-sixth Avenue. Smoke comes out of its exhaust pipe. You can guess what it reminds me of. And a little water drips from it too. The L Taraval slides by smoothly. It's heading downhill toward the Great Highway where fog makes sand and sea and sky into one flat white canvas upon which to paint the rest of the day. Fog eliminates the distinguishing characteristics, and everything blends together.

Faces look out at me from the Coors Lite can-color cars of the Muni train. Mostly old, this time of day. Mostly Asian. Something unsettling in their blank expressions. Reminds me of a documentary I once saw on Auschwitz. Of death camps. And how those rides must've been. Knowing that you are going to die. I feel something then. Maybe regret. I study the storefronts across the way: Okazu Ya Sushi and Rapid Refund and Total Life Health Foods. I sip my cup of coffee thinking now it's a real drink I need.

My head hurts and I close my eyes.

***

When I open my eyes, I'm somewhere else and everybody

in the room is naked. A girl I do not recognize grinds in my lap and tells me I'm too fucking skinny. She has a Russian name. She has a Russian accent. I give her money. Most of it. I don't even know how much. She rolls a hundred-dollar bill, hoovers a line of the white powder up her nose.

***

Later that same night I am sitting on a stool that squeaks. The man next to me says his name is Thor. What the fuck. He says he's a professional gambler. He says it's like playing the stock market. He says he's looking for some action. He says he's also a hunting guide from Alaska who shoots big game for rich young gluttons. Bullshit.

I'm calling bullshit on you, I say.

Then I order a shot of Fernet Branca so I can blackout again.

I prefer to think of it as time travel.

It's my only superpower, the ability to shut my eyes and then I open them and I'm on the other side of town or in the backseat of a car or one time on a flight to Vegas.

Thor tells me he'll drop a disease-ridden bear from thirty yards and convince some pasty-faced CEO that it's a good fucking kill. Then the CEO will get a big hard on and stuff his prize and mount it on the wall of his ten thousand square foot den in Atherton. He'll brag to his bros. Thor tells me they can't hit the broad side of a barn.

Not these dot commers, he says. Not fish in a barrel.

The bullshitter keeps bullshitting because that's what they do.

I stop paying attention. Put my shot away and close my eyes.

Because that's what I do.

***

I take a girl named Lila to Candlestick Park. The Niners are going to get smoked by the Browns. I punch this one guy for wearing a Tim Couch jersey at the tailgate before the game. Some dark-skinned brother from the Double Rock housing projects is selling caps and visors and long sleeve t-shirts, and I buy Lila a lid for five dollars and she kisses me and wears it backwards. She has never been to a professional sporting event before.

We drink Jell-O shots with Mike the Electrician and Sal and Tony Dry Wall. They barbecue and I hollow out the roll for my tri-tip sandwich so I can sneak a half pint of Jack Daniels past the guards. It's ninety-seven degrees in the shade and Sal cuts the legs off his jeans with the knife he always carries. Tony Dry Wall makes ceviche and ribs and he shares his barrel-aged tequila. There are ice-cold beers for everybody, and somebody fires up a two-stroke margarita mixer that sounds like a chainsaw and you can smell the fumes of it. Mike the Electrician has brought a Nerf football and I toss it around with his young son. The boy has a natural athletic ability that I find refreshing somehow.

Sal sits with Lila on foldout chairs under a tree. He tells her about the old days before he owned a chain of restaurants. Sal and Tony used to rumble with West Portal gangs in the sand dunes by Giannini where they ended up building Saint Ignatius. Back when they wore leather jackets. Sal explains that if you ran with a group of right guys and were willing to throw hands now and again then you were going to get some pussy and that's why they did it. Not like this half-crazy motherfucker, he says, indicating me.

This guy just can't help himself, Sal says. A born fighter.

Still does it for fun.

He doesn't necessarily paint a romantic picture of my past for her. Sal has always been more of a diplomat, but he can bring it when he wants, I remember. Lila says that she sees a whole other side of me after talking to Sal and watching me play catch with Mike's boy. She puts her hand in my hair, closes her eyes and smiles at the blue sky.

See, I'm a broken man for the most part but my medicine is still strong.

We have lower-reserve tickets that are only in the sun for part of the first quarter, but it doesn't matter because it is unusually hot. Oakland is burning and ashes fall like flakes of snow. Then we run out of water and even ice for sodas, so I keep drinking beer because I need something cold. An old man in our section passes out from heat stroke and the paramedics hustle him off on a stretcher. The Niners keep trying to run up the middle and of course they keep getting stuffed. They can't score a touchdown even when they are in the red zone, but the new field goal kicker earns his pay. The Browns score two touchdowns late to the Niners' four early field goals and so Cleveland is up by two with less than a minute left on the game clock. My mind is taking me to that bad place where my friend Sal was trying to make a play at Lila back at the tailgate. Deep down I know it's not true and Sal is a standup guy, but alcohol is not always my best counsel.

And somebody must pay for the way that I feel.

There's a Cleveland fan in front of me who won't sit down or keep his trap shut so after Jeff Garcia's fourth-quarter interception I turn him around with one hand and sock him hard enough in the nose with the other that it busts open and sprays blood on me and Lila, and the dude's on queer street for sure with wobbly legs and all, and security comes and then the real police. Lila cries and I finish my beer and laugh, I don't bother to resist. I tell Lila to find Sal or Tony for a safe ride home. Lock me up, boys, I say to the cops. Lock me up before I wreck everything else and really hurt somebody.

moon

ask of wind

make us walk

pull our voices

smell of Route 101 traffic

dirty my ears

loud & louder

the city moon

is an empty spoon

~eskimo

SOME BABY

Doc craves solitude more than anything today, so he smokes a joint near Stow Lake. Eyes closed, fretting over losing custody of his kids, when a black and tan Rottweiler crashes through a shrub and bites him on the calf. Really latches on. Out of nowhere. It hardly breaks the skin because of his pants but he puts two bullets in the dog's melon just out of principle. He's not much for firearms but he's holding a nine for his pal Sloop again. Other than that, he had been minding his own fucking business for once in his life.

The lady who was walking the dog until it broke free cries.

It's my baby, she says.

Some baby.

She calls the dog Zeus and rocks that big, dying beast in her cradled arms while his blood drizzles onto the sidewalk like motor oil leaking from a car engine. The scene reminds Doc of something, but he can't remember exactly what. High as a kite now.

My husband's going to kill me, the lady says.

Doc tells her there's a leash law in Golden Gate Park in case she didn't know. Especially for such an unpredictable breed. She cries some more. Doc slips the nine back in his pants. Jesus, he says. He digs a Xanax out of his pocket and puts it on his tongue.

Why'd you do him like that, she says.

Doc swallows the pill. Why what, he says.

She's just another stupid bitch obviously and there is no reasoning with people like her, he figures. Doc leaves before the cops can show up and ask him about the gun or what the fuck he was doing in the park in the first place. He wants to see Lisa, but she needs privacy to be with her sickness. Asked him to stay away until the end of the day.

He's not sure he can wait that long now, after this little incident.

He needs the fleeting sense of comfort that only she can give him.

The lady puts the corpse down gently in a patch of grass and clover and she tries to follow Doc. Calls after him and when that doesn't work, she yells into her cell phone. She's right on his ass. She isn't making any sense because she's still caught up in the moment of the thing. Whoever is on the other end is trying to calm her down and figure out what's going on by the sounds of it, and she has to stop to breathe and count to ten. It's probably her fucking faggot-ass husband that she said is going to murder her.

Doc makes a break for it. He doesn't want her to get his plate number, so he ducks into the woods to wait it out. She's scared to go past the first line of trees and he can't say he blames her one bit. She's babbling again. He's gone, she says. He did it and now I can't find him, she says. She uses words like crazy and gangster and thug to describe him. He holds his breath. After a few minutes, she stops poking around. That makes Doc happy because he's willing to go to the next level but only if absolutely necessary. He'd sworn to himself the last time that he'd never go back inside. Not if he can help it. Not over something stupid and senseless like a crazy dog. He stays hidden until it's all quiet.

After he's sure she's gone he walks casually to Angelo's old El Camino that almost doesn't start but finally turns over on the third try. It's a real piece of shit, but he's borrowing it while Angelo is in lockup for violating several conditions of his parole. The muffler has a hole but that is the least of his problems right now. He drives to Angelo's home. He uses the term loosely. There's parking right out front, which is unheard of in the Outer Richmond District and so he takes it as a good sign but doesn't really put too much stock into that kind of nonsense. Fate and shit. Considers himself a realist. It's just pure luck is all. That's his frame of mind. Lisa is unconscious on Angelo's couch, which is normal for a Sunday. She always tells Doc that Angelo is like a weight around her neck, dragging her down. Even though he is banging her behind his best friend's back, it hurt Doc at first to hear her put it into words like that, the fact that Angelo had gone from being a world-beater to that guy, a has-been who never even was, but Doc knows it is the truth. He puts ice cubes against where the Rott's teeth left several small red-raised marks.

His goal was to end the thing with Lisa today.

To tell her how he only gets supervised visits with his kids now. The family court judge said according to his case worker he wasn't in a position to provide a healthy living environment for children. Whatever the fuck that means. But the upshot is he's got to fly right for a while and get his shit together, and part of that is to stop messing with Lisa.

He doesn't think she's going to take the news well.

Hoping for the best but certainly expecting the worst.

She had long ago promised to slice off his balls with a spoon if he ever ditched her. She has a tendency to get depressed and uses prescription pills and of course sleep is the second-best thing. There's an empty bottle of Johnnie Walker Red on the floor near where her arm is stretched out. Doc tries not to wake her. Makes himself an egg sandwich with bacon and cheese and homemade salsa. Puts the nine in the cookie jar under some stale Oreos. Sits in a metal foldout chair and chows down. Watches her sleep. She's still damn pretty. In her restless state of reverie, she twitches like a pup. He hops in the shower to see if that will change his outlook. It doesn't but at least he's clean now.

Then Lisa still hasn't budged.

Doc fears the worst and laughs out loud until she opens her eyes at him and then he puts his fingers to his lips and hushes in a soothing gesture. He needs fixing and he kneels beside her and slides his hand under the blanket. She's wearing one of Angelo's wife beaters and a soft pair of cotton briefs. She's already hot and wet down there. Doc drops his towel on the floor while she tugs her panties down and kicks them away. Then he gets inside her from behind and moves slowly, rhythmically, the way she likes. She says his name, but he closes his eyes and pictures some random whore, tries to recall some random whore scent. Then the apartment is suddenly jarred and every piece of secondhand furniture rattles and creaks. Doc opens his eyes and Lisa gets on top of him.

Earthquake, he says, but Lisa doesn't hear him.

She is oblivious to the new danger that surrounds them. Intense, focused, concentrating on her center. Her eyes are closed but Doc watches the walls move like paper or bed sheets hanging on a clothesline. Somewhere deep beneath the earth two tectonic plates are shifting slightly and despite the brief release the tension between them will remain. And there will be aftershocks. Doc considers it but one of the risks of continuing to hang around this damn place. Lisa digs her nails into his chest when she finishes, sirens outside getting closer, and she rolls off him onto her side. Jesus Christ, she says. Puts her hand on his heart. Doc extends his legs and turns his head away from her, and through the open window he can smell the fog-damp streets of San Francisco.

crave

on the ninth day in Spain
            Tuesday
the smell made her sick

there was nothing inside

she brought him tea when he
asked

boiled

she faced the wall
with her fingers in her ears
~ eskimo

DON'T CALL IT FRISCO

Charlie spends the night at 850 Bryant for a minor infraction involving fisticuffs. He says it wasn't bad. He laughs about it, of course. Gooch apologizes for not being around for bail, but Charlie isn't worried. He doesn't take things personally. They ride over to Dubliner for some hair of the dog that bit them. Rogan is there and Hang Dog Sally and Mike Shelly and Gay Phil. Phil is an accountant and known weekend cross dresser.

Phil is worried about Gooch's portfolio because it's taking a beating from stock market volatility. They're sitting in the corner near the broken jukebox. Phil is leaning back against the electronic dartboard and there is a dead cockroach stuck through with one of the darts so it's situated smack in the bull's eye. We need to shift away from equities, Phil says.

Whatever.

More bonds.

Fine.

Money markets and the like.

All right, Gooch says.

Get away from financial services and international exposure.

Listen, just do what you do.

Yeah, we're really getting killed there.

It's all Greek to Gooch. But Gay Phil is pushing, clearly nervous about something. Sweat building on his forehead. All that credit noise, he says.

Gooch sips his drink and stares into space. He figures his pal is skimming, maybe some kind of Ponzi scheme he has going.

We're just getting shit on right now, Phil says. Then he can see that he's losing Gooch with all the money talk. Nowhere to hide right now but it'll turn around, he says.

All fucking right then.

We dropped a sizable chunk already, Phil says.

There, he said it, and Gooch didn't even flinch.

Just go ahead and do your thing, Phil. I trust you.

Gay Phil makes a face like he just got socked in the kidney. All right, he says.

You know.

Yeah, I'll draw up some papers for you to sign.

Papers.

For the transfer of funds. We can move some shit around.

Whatever, Gooch says. Do what you do.

I've got some good mutual funds picked out that will be a good safe haven.

Safe haven.

That's right, just someplace to park it until the dust settles.

All right then, Gooch says. I like the idea of a safe haven.

It's just cycles.

Cycles.

Yeah, these things go in cycles and you simply have to ride them out sometimes.

All right.

But no sense in taking a bath if you don't have to, Gay Phil says.

Right.

Be happy I already had you spread out.

I'm real happy. Believe you me. Don't I look happy.

We'd be up a real creek without a paddle if you know what I mean.

Get the papers for me, Phil.

Okay.

I'll sign them.

Gooch takes his Ketel over ice and sits at a table by himself. He sees Charlie put his hand on Hang Dog Sally's leg. Rogan is getting pissed about it. The money isn't a big deal to him. For years, for every dollar he made wrenching on cars he gave fifty cents to Phil to invest for him. Gooch never had any use for the money before and now he wouldn't know what to do with it anyhow. He doesn't like to talk about it. He hasn't even told his fiancé yet. He figures he'll surprise her. This nut could be their chance to get away, start somewhere with a clean slate. Maybe somewhere up north in the country where an old guy who can fix old cars can earn a decent living. Near a river. He closes his eyes and thinks about what that would be like. He can almost hear the river running.

Hey, Gooch, what you think, Rogan says.

Gooch opens his eyes and looks at Rogan.

About what, he says.

Used to be I could tell a fag by how he dressed.

Yeah.

But these young guys today all dress like fags.

Yeah, these kids dress different now.

Not that I care, but your boy here, Rogan says, indicating Charlie.

Gooch looks at Charlie.

He says the city is being over-run and gentrified by these types, Rogan says.

I said yuppified, Charlie says.

All right then, Rogan says. Yuppified.

He looks at Gooch. What do you say, Gooch, he says, in defense of our fair city.

Shit, Gooch says, fair to who exactly.

Well, we got a roof over our head don't we, Rogan says.

All right, I'll give you that.

And we got this nice young man pouring our drinks.

Amen to that.

They raise their glasses to Murph behind the stick and take a drink.

But, really, Gooch, what's your take.

Fuck. Overrun isn't quite right but certainly there's a new element.

A new element.

First, we had the beatniks, then the hippies, yuppies, hipsters and now the fucking little tech bros are taking over, Hang Dog Sally says, practically into her empty glass.

Our esteemed professor with a history lesson, Rogan says.

They're taking over Frisco, she says.

Don't call it Frisco. You can't call it that.

I'm from here, you sonofabitch.

I didn't know that was the rule, if you were born here you can call it that.

It's like only blacks can call each other nigger.

Jesus.

Yeah, so a new element that seems to be everywhere, Gooch says.

Everywhere, Rogan says and slams his empty glass on the bar. See, that's the kind of horse shit we get from Gooch when he finally opens his fucking mouth. Everywhere.

He shoves his stool back and stands up to his full height. He's a big man.

Philosophy, he says. Is that all you got for me tonight, boy.

He faces Gooch.

There's a place down the road you can go with that shit, he says. Unless you got something else for me.

Gooch puts his hands over his face. They smell like the tranny of the 1979 Camaro he'd been working on all day. He opens them up peek-a-boo style and Rogan is still there. Shit, Gooch says, I thought maybe I was having another one of those dreams.

Rogan looks confused but he doesn't step back.

Gooch had sensed trouble brewing and now here it is. He can see that Rogan is trying to make some sort of stand and doesn't really blame him for that. He pictures putting his friend through the plate-glass window. He puts down his drink and stands up to do it but Murph intervenes in the sensible and diplomatic fashion that Gooch has always appreciated about him, and Charlie is hungry anyhow. They leave out of there and Charlie buys Gooch a chicken burrito from El Toreador and they walk to the Philosopher's Club. Josh is behind the bar there. He won't do a shot of Fernet with them because he's training for the Alcatraz triathlon or some such shit. He's always training now. Charlie says that Rogan was just pissed because Sally is a two-bit whore.

That's why he was talking crazy, Charlie says. I was working on his girl a bit.

Yeah. I saw that.

So, he was trying to stir shit up.

Yup.

You know how he gets.

Yeah. I know how he gets.

He was egging you on, Charlie says.

Yeah, he was really asking for it there.

That was good how you handled it.

Shit, I've been knowing him my whole life, Gooch says.

Well, I'd of slugged him.

No, you wouldn't either.

No, you're right, Charlie says. Not Rogan I wouldn't.

***

Fast Freddy is drinking a forty at Ocean Beach. He played fullback at SF State. That was before the service and way before Lompoc. Gooch almost doesn't recognize him because he's wearing his hair in dreadlocks now. What the fuck, Gooch says. It's hot and tourists are down there too. They're mostly watching the surfers slipping the tubes. Fast Freddy takes off his t-shirt and he has not gone soft at all. He has the brand of a black fraternity on his right biceps. There are a couple bohemian types he is rapping to and Gooch listens to him run his game for a while. He hasn't lost a step. They smoke a little reefer that somebody is passing around. It's pretty green. The McNulty brothers walk by with their thick-shouldered pit bull and they stop and shake Gooch's hand. They talk some shit about nigger this and nigger that and Fast Freddy is getting agitated, so Gooch tells the twins to get lost.

They didn't mean nothing by it, he says after they split.

I know.

They're half stupid anyhow.

Only half.

Gooch laughs.

Whatever.

It can get plenty rough down there. Everybody trying to

beat the heat. Too many opposites in one place. The Sunset Boys and Mission Street and Daly City. Lots of posturing but Gooch just lays back and watches. Fast Freddy is folding towels at the Central YMCA. It isn't much but it keeps him out of trouble. He's trying to get on with the fire department like everybody else. He took the written test down at Moscone Center and is waiting to hear his score. Gooch tells him he'll have to lose the dreads if he gets in and Fast Freddy laughs. Gooch walks to the liquor store to get more beer and a bottle.

John John Kelly is wearing a Ben Davis with only the top button done, Sunset District Incorporated style; SDI was rough as shit back in the day but most of the original guys have gone spiritual. There's a picture of Jesus on John John's abdomen that he likes to show off. It isn't bad for an amateur job he got in the joint. He drinks with Gooch and Fast Freddy for a little while and they talk about all the sweet meat out on the promenade. Freddy is happy to reflect on old times with a couple guys who had been there too. Abby comes by, a neighborhood gal, but she's poison and liable to get somebody shot in the face. Her shoulders are sunburned. Gooch can smell how desperate she is for a fix.

The four of them end up at John John's apartment to do some blow and the men each take turns with her on the couch with the others right there and some porn on a laptop screen. She cries after, says she feels like a whore, and Fast Freddy laughs and tells her she isn't a whore because they aren't going to pay her. John John zips his fly and tells her not to worry because she couldn't sell that ass if she wanted. Abby goes from sad to angry and throws a porcelain statue of Buddha and it breaks into pieces on the floor.

***

On the anniversary of Johnny Cash's death, Gooch raises his glass up high. He saw him quote Roy Orbison in an interview on television one time. Johnny said that Roy said that rocks are rocks and diamonds are diamonds, but men are made of good and bad.

Phil the cross-dressing accountant takes Gooch to a sex club. Not his scene but his fiancé is working night shift and he's bored and lonely. Phil has more papers for him to sign anyhow. Phil is wearing women's clothes and makeup tonight, but no amount of blush will cover up the fact that he is a man. He pays the door charge and the guy on the stool smiles at him but looks Gooch up and down, head to toe evaluation. The place reminds Gooch of what he's heard of the bathhouses of the early 1980s before Feinstein shut them down as a public health emergency and her fight against AIDS and STDs and drug abuse. The inside is dim and it literally smells like shit. An awful stench.

Phil explains about the smell. That it's a turn on for some people. They take a dump on each other as part of the foreplay. Gooch is open minded, but he doesn't understand that at all. Not even for a minute. He thinks about Liz Fontana and all that she puts up with on the job. Some twisted fucks in this world. He feels sick for a minute.

There are these little rooms and cubbies that you can use. Phil leaves him alone for a while so he can hook up with some boy toy he's just discovered. Gooch finds a comfortable place to sit and almost everybody leaves him alone. He just wants to check it out and see what goes on. Everybody's on poppers it seems and you can smell that too.

It's mostly gays and curious tech bros and young women maybe trying to hitch to their wagons. This one gal wearing a halter top that says Contents Under Pressure. She approaches Gooch, says she likes his new tattoo. He pushes up his shirt sleeve and turns his arm so she can get the full effect. Her name is Rebecca and she's a regular at the club.

She's high as fuck, that much is certain, and recognizes that Gooch is in a far-away place too and they sit like that only talking a little bit about the local weather patterns and listening to curtains open and close and occasional moans and slurps and the sounds of dry friction. Rebecca wants Gooch to walk with her, so he does. The lighting throughout the place makes everything soft and red. The music is that funky techno beat.

Rebecca introduces Gooch to her friend named Henry who likes to watch.

Henry wants to watch us, she says.

So that's their game. Gooch isn't sure about it at first, but Henry is older and harmless and probably can't even get it up anymore. They go into one of the little cubbies and she undoes his fly and he lifts her skirt and turns her around and puts his hands around her throat, squeezing, and once inside her he hardly moves a muscle and she barely does either. All the way inside, she says. Gooch pushes deeper and they stand there like that, unable to see each other's faces, eyes open, attached in that way. Swaying a little bit to the heavy bass coming from the wireless speakers. Lasts for a few minutes.

Henry thanks Gooch when they're done, he says it was awkward and beautiful and surreal, and at the same moment Phil texts that he is waiting in the lobby. Rebecca smiles goodbye and for some reason Gooch feels compelled to tell her about Johnny Cash. Tells her about rocks and that the man in black understood there were bad parts of himself that he had to come to terms with. Wait, we didn't do nothing wrong here, she says, straightening her skirt and dismissing him with an upward flick of her hand.

***

Phil is already sitting in the Uber with the windows down when Gooch hits the curb and then from the backseat of the Lincoln Navigator he watches a homeless man, bloodied and naked as the day he was born, run up the block and turn the corner onto South Van Ness. There is no sense of urgency in his movement. Looks like he's just going for a jog. Perfect form. Runners arms. Gooch tracks him until they take the freeway onramp. He leans back against his seat and wonders where the man had left his clothes and whose blood he was covered in anyhow. The driver looks at him for a second through the rearview mirror and then without a word he turns the radio to a hip-hop station. The vehicle smells like armpits and cheap cologne. Phil's lipstick is smudged and his wig is crooked. Gooch closes his eyes, thinking it's too cold to be running around town naked.

blackout

I was drunk
&

forgetting things

& falling

down &

we both
hated me
then
~ eskimo

THE GOOD KIND

When I got back from Mexico she was pissed. She sat in a cold jail for six whole days because the drugs were in the house that was in her name. They put our kids in foster care. She got fired from her teaching job. Her old man drove down from San Pablo to bail her out. He called me a fucking pendejo. I stayed with Chapo until things cooled off.

She phoned me on my cell and said she wanted a divorce. And she was taking the kids. Over my dead body, but I didn't say it out loud. She called me a fucking drug dealer. She called me worse things than that. I let her give me an earful because I felt bad.

The truth is, I would never let her leave me. Not on those terms.

I told her to sit tight and not make any hasty decisions. Chapo let me borrow his Thunderbird and I floored it down 80. The kids were back home and they were excited to see me except for Junior because he was old enough to understand what was going on. The others hugged my legs and Maria threw a frying pan at me. She'd been making my favorite papooses, and chicken and jamon and cheese spilled all over me along with hot oil. Chapo was always surprised at the shit I let her get away with.

I didn't want to hit her.

Then she cleaned up and used the first aid kit where my arm was cooked. Junior got it from the bathroom. He was a studious and obedient boy.

***

Later I told Junior to watch the niños for a while so I could talk to his mother in private. He smart assed me because he thought he was a little man already. It made me proud of him, but I still had to show him that he wasn't quite ready for that yet. Then he cried but it was the good kind of cry that doesn't really come out. And there was fear in his eyes, but it was the good kind of fear that every son should feel toward his father.

There was rain on Mission Street. We fogged the windows of the Thunderbird with our words. I parked on Twenty Fourth near the BART station and McDonald's. There was a street musician banging bongo drums and a vendor taking a break from selling coconut palettas. He scowled with fat owl eyes and smoked half a cigarette.

She described how they strip searched her, humiliated her. As she spoke it was clear that they had been able to break her down, to get her to say too much, using the kids as leverage. I needed to know exactly what. Then I explained the consequences. She tapped on my chest with her closed fists until I'd had enough.

Enough, I said.

She called me a fucking puto. She said she couldn't live this way anymore. I put my hand over her mouth. Hard at first, to shut her up so I could think, come up with a plan, and then soft and I worked my index finger around her perfect lips and the inside of her cheek that was already moist and warm, ready for me. She bit my thumb in a playful way and then she exhaled and put her wrists behind my neck and pulled me toward her.

Ah yes, I whispered, this is how it will always go.

Then she pushed me away like she was having second thoughts. Then she tugged at the beltline of my jeans and climbed on my lap and stuffed me inside her and we bumped up against each other for a few long minutes. Then her back arched against the steering wheel with the suicide knob. My face was on the flesh of her chest and the small gold cross she always wore. She smelled like the caramelized sugar you drizzle over flan.

Afterward we just sat there sticking to each other and breathing.

She said the worst part was that it was going on her permanent record. And she said that her old man and her tios and her four brothers wanted to run me out of town, but I laughed and told her they didn't have the cojones for it. Not one complete set among them. She shot me a bitter sideways glance. She didn't like to hear it, but she knew it was true. There are two kinds of men and I was one and they were the other. I told her she'd better talk some sense into them before they did something crazy and regrettable.

I had to get the car back to Chapo. She stared at the plastic dashboard. There was music. That rancheras shit that Chapo liked. He could be such a fucking wetback sometimes. But when the chips were down, he was my carnal. Like for something like this. He'd take care of all the details so I would not get my hands dirty. I stroked her hair and called her my little salvatrucha.

She smiled half a smile. I think she knew.

She asked me to come inside and say goodbye to the kids, but I wanted to beat the traffic. That's what I told her. There was a moment of silence between us that hung heavy like a dusty old manta. Then she got out and held her jacket over her head and tried to dodge the drops that were falling faster now. Her wet skirt was clinging to her ass and she splashed in a puddle. Now when I close my eyes tight, I can remember her just like that.

with me

it
is all right
when
he
is with me

for

no other reason
than
that
~ eskimo

LUCKY THE LIMO

Lucky drives the limo into a ditch. It isn't actually a ditch, more of a muddy hole on the edge of a construction site behind the ballpark on Third Street in China Basin. He hears they're building a billion square feet for the UCSF Medical Center. He doesn't mean to do it but falls asleep behind the wheel. A couple drunks in the back seat making out.

Sometimes to make a little extra scratch and if Marco has him in hover mode, he'll scoop up a fare or two off the books. Cruise up and down Broadway watching people pouring out of bars and getting sick of waiting for taxi cabs. Eventually somebody will wave him over and he'll quote a flat rate of fifty bucks. He's open to haggling, but Jesus Christ, the gas prices today. That's always his line. Then he'll pocket the cash and charge the gasoline to Marco when he fills up the tank. He was Uber before there was Uber.

The drunks are not wearing seatbelts and they get jostled around pretty good when the limo ends up in the muddy hole.

What the fuck, the man says.

Get our money back, the woman says.

Lucky tastes blood. His lip is cut. Good thing the air bag doesn't work, he thinks.

Hey man, you could of killed us, the man says.

Is he driving drunk, the woman says.

Lucky unharnesses himself, opens his door and gets out

to assess the situation. A basic nose-dive. Damage to the grill and front bumper, and the driver side fender is crumpled like paper. Flat tire. Radiator leaking green fluid and hissing, hot and busted. Fuck me, he thinks. Marco is going to be motherfucking pissed about this one for sure.

Didn't you see the fence, the man says.

Lucky doesn't feel the need to say shit to either one of these assholes.

All those fucking signs, the man says.

The limo had crashed right through that fence. And one of those signs is on the roof of the car. The man and the woman must climb out through a rear window as the back doors are pinned against dirt. Her skirt rips a bit when it gets snagged on the undercarriage, she slips and stumbles in the mud. Starts to cry. A real fucking mess here.

Make him give us our money back, she says.

The man helps her out of the hole. She takes her heels off and stands there holding them by the straps. Hey man, you could of killed us, the man says again.

Lucky looks at the guy. He spits blood. No fucking way, he thinks.

Honey.

All right, so like, give us the fifty bucks back.

Lucky tells him to fuck off. He tells the woman to fuck off, too.

I'm only out here cause of you two, he says.

What the fuck.

Your fault as much as mine, he says.

The man starts to back off, but the woman isn't going to

give up that easy, Lucky can see that as plain as day. Honey, she says to the man.

The man starts to say something and so Lucky shows him the gun he used to shoot the Iranian last week, that thieving prick. He should've tossed the gun in the bay like Marco told him, but having it makes him feel brave and strong. The man's face turns white and his sphincter probably tightens a little. The woman doesn't say anything either and Lucky figures that right there was worth the price of admission.

Listen, Lucky says.

The man looks at him.

We got us a pretty messy situation here, Lucky says.

The man moves closer to the woman.

But I got this here under control, Lucky says.

The woman makes a face at the man.

You two should go on home now, Lucky says. Trying to make it sound like he's doing them a solid. Cops get here, they could cite you for a drunk in public, he says.

Shit, the woman says.

At least fifty bucks more for that and maybe put you in the clink, he says.

Reaching for straws now.

The woman wants to say something smart but holds her tongue.

Back there you can catch a bus or a train, he says. Get an Uber or Lyft.

Fuck that and fuck you, the woman says. She doesn't much believe the gun.

Cabs come by too on their way to the onramp, Lucky says.

He tells them to cross Lefty O'Doul Bridge and hang a left at the statue of Willie Mays. They start walking. Then they stop so the woman can put her heels back on. She holds onto the man's shoulder. He looks back at Lucky and shakes his head from side to side as though maybe trying to get his courage up. Lucky gives him the thousand-yard stare and practically sees dude's tail go between his legs. Then he watches them walk away. At least they're sober now, he thinks. And I gave them a good story to tell their kids someday. A character-building experience. Probably going to get mugged though. Oh well, I bet she's packing mace. His conscience is clear as far as he is concerned.

Lucky hates to call Marco so late with this type of thing to report. Especially since it is his night off and he has taken one of the girls to eat frog legs in Belden Place. Trying to wine and dine her even though Lucky had advised his boss against it. Don't shit where you eat, he'd said. Partly believing his advice but also hoping to give the new girl a shot at the title his own damn self. Lucky knows an old broad who's staying on a houseboat nearby. He can walk over there and spend the night. Maybe relive some old memories. Report the limo stolen. Take a screwdriver to the key lock and ignition to make it look authentic. Tell Marco, yeah, I just ran inside Little Darlings for a minute because some yahoos were knocking over chairs again. Stupid motherfuckers we got to deal with. Ban their sorry asses from the club, he'll recommend. When he came back out the limo was gone from the yellow, he'll say. Probably some hood rats from the projects joyriding.

He works it out in his head as he walks, the big lie, the story he's going to tell. The bay water is black and sloshing against the thick round posts of the dock. Gull shit and cigarette butts and rusted hibachis, and at the far end an eight-hundred-pound sea lion asleep and snoring. Lucky remembers the sea lion. He's been frequenting the houseboat moorings for many years. Most of them sun at Pier 39 but this is an odd one. Comes out only at night and enjoys human contact and other than that keeps to himself. Beverly Hills has taken to calling him Han Solo because he's always alone. Lucky is looking forward to seeing Beverly. Maybe after a quick toss she'll give him a free haircut.

***

Joey is never going to live this one down. And things had been going pretty good with Sheila lately. She was on his case less about shit it seemed. But now this. He knows for a fact she will hold onto this one. The heel on her left shoe is busted so she must limp to keep up with him. In his ear hole the entire time. Holding her phone in front of her face, trying to get Uber or Lyft. That was really fucking beautiful, she says.

He rolls his eyes at her.

Your performance back there, she says, tapping away at the little screen.

Joey tries to ignore her.

You really outdid yourself, she says.

They cross the bridge.

My fucking hero, she says.

Hang a left at Willie Mays.

Really, she says.

She can't believe that Joey let that limo driver basically steal their money. Not to mention that he nearly killed them. This takes the cake, she thinks. Practically shit his pants when he saw the gun. Unbelievable, her luck with men in this damn town.

Aren't you just a little bit ashamed, she says.

Joey imagines her dead in the limo back there.

Please tell me you're a little bit ashamed at least, she says.

He doesn't say anything, has nothing to say, really.

Please tell me that, she says.

Joey pictures her floating face down in the bay.

Because that would be something, she says.

Fuck.

That would be a start, she says. Like admitting you have a problem.

He can't shake the image of her pinned beneath the back tires of the stretch.

That'd be a sign you're maybe growing a pair, she says. I could work with that.

Even at this hour the ballpark smells like garlic fries. They had been on their way to the place she rents on Ripley Street in the Bernal Heights but now he just wants to go home. Alone. Tired of all this. He speeds up a little and she takes her shoes off again. A yellow cab is stopped at the red light at Second Street. The blinker indicates it's going to turn toward the 280 South on-ramp. If they cross the street in time, he can pick them up no problem. Joey waves his hands and starts to jog. Sheila barely keeps up with him. The driver sees them and pulls over. They get in. He looks over his shoulder at Joey.

So, I'm going home, Joey says to Sheila.

Oh fuck, all right then, whatever, let's go there, she says.

No, I mean you should go to your place, too.

What the fuck.

Listen.

No, you listen you cocksucker.

See, I don't need this.

The driver is bored but he waits.

What you need is a motherfucking spine, she says.

Here we go again.

That's right here we go again, she says. You gutless wonder.

Jesus.

Because you never cease to amaze me, she says.

Joey tells the driver Sheila's address and cross street, recommends taking Portero Hill exit off the freeway and then turning left on Alabama Street, gives him some cash to cover the ride. Gets out of the car and shuts the door.

You fucking faggot, Sheila says through her halfway open window.

Joey waves goodbye.

Leaving me in here with Osama fucking bin Laden, she says.

The driver smiles. Joey closes the door. She opens the window more so she can share a final thought or two. You fucking chickenshit piece of shit motherfucker, she says. The driver flashes his gold tooth, guns the engine and the cab roars away, and Sheila's curses trail it like the white smoke pluming from the exhaust pipe.

Then they're gone.

Joey feels good for the first time that night. He lets out a long breath that he can see. His bones are cold and he shivers. He notices that he's been sweating—his dress shirt is soaked through. They'd been dancing at the Bubble Lounge all night, drinking apple martinis. He walks along the Embarcadero past Red's Java House and the Hi Dive and Pier 23 where they have salsa night every Thursday and Joey got his nose broken once. A tugboat chugs beneath the Bay Bridge. Stars visible through a slight crack in the fog. Deep bass of the horn warning ships away from the rocky Northern California coast.

Hey man, you got some change.

Joey hadn't even noticed the black guy until he spoke. He rabbit ears his pockets. Sorry bro, he says.

How about you want to buy this movie. The guy has a porn movie, the old VHS style, in the original packaging but all beat up. I'll give you this for ten bucks, he says.

No, sorry.

It's real good.

Sorry man.

Five then.

Hey.

Lots of that young pussy you like.

Thanks, but I couldn't even play that if I wanted to.

The guy tucks the movie back up under his long shirt. Looks around, nervous. All right, God bless, he says without making any further eye contact.

The guy is probably a heroin addict. Joey has read about them. He watches him slip back into the shadows. Probably a whole entire camp of them around here somewhere, he figures. Junk City or something. Probably not the smartest move to be walking around alone down here in the middle of the night, he thinks. And his very next thought is, Jesus Christ maybe I am a big fucking pussy. That's how deep Sheila is in his head now.

He has always thought of himself as non-confrontational and sensible, but he's beginning to question himself, thanks to her. Maybe she's right. There's nothing to be scared of, he thinks. And just then he hears a wet thud like if you're trying to bust open a ripe melon with a wood mallet. He sees stars and his knees buckle and he falls to the ground, on his back. He can't move but he's still conscious, eyes wide open. The guy with the video is standing over him with another guy, the one with the piece of rebar.

He's on queer street for sure.

Did you see his legs.

Check his pockets.

Video guy checks his pockets while rebar guy keeps his eyes peeled.

Here's his wallet.

They spill the contents onto the sidewalk.

Shit, he broke as a spoke.

Rebar guy puts the little bit of cash in his sock. Blood is pooling around Joey's head. Oh man, you look at that.

It ain't no coming back.

Is he got a cell.

Video guy comes up with Joey's cell phone.

Call 911 and tell them he's bleeding bad and then let's get gone.

Video guy punches in the numbers and waits. Yeah, white dude gone to bleed out less you get here quick. He listens. Rebar guy looks around nervously. Nah, I ain't got time for that. He listens and looks around again. Justin Herman or thereabouts, he says.

He drops the cell phone and they split.

***

Joey watches them hobble into the deeper shadows like funky old haunts. Gentle waves off the bay lap at the cement walls of the promenade. Darkness rushes in to fill the spaces between the square concrete tubes of Vaillancourt Fountain, that massive geometrical octopus upon whose tentacles Bono spray painted *Rock N Roll Stops the Traffic* and Mayor Feinstein got her panties in a bunch back in 1987. Joey remembers the free concert that was billed as *Save the Yuppies*. His dad took him and his sis just before everything went to shit. Riding high on the old man's shoulders that day. Joey feels warm and smells piss and wonders if it's his own. He closes his eyes and whispers. *Sleight of hand and twist of fate. On a bed of nails, she makes me wait. And I wait, without you.*

ocean

wind

runs

along the beach

time

rhymes

& shadows

teach

birds

dance

from water's reach

we

flee

from both

or each

~ eskimo

TWO RULES

She only had two rules and I broke both. This should be a love story instead of what it is. I was that excited about the way things were going. And if you knew me, you'd know that I'm not one to toss the L-word around too much. I need my freedom. You know what I'm talking about. But I was willing to give all that up for Mercedes. That was her name. Yeah. Like the car. So, of course, my opening line to her was: Let me drive. Get it. I don't know how I come up with this stuff so fast. It just comes to me. It's a gift and I thank God for it. Thank you, God. As you can imagine, I got her with that one. Hook, line and sinker. Thought I was the funniest thing since, well, I can't think of what right now because I'm a little nervous in this setting. You understand. But you get my point. Mitchell Brothers was packed but it was like it was just me and her all alone in there. So, to answer your question, that's how we first met, and I must admit I was happy with the way the relationship was progressing. I can't believe I just said that.

So, I was throwing caution to the wind and jumping right in. First time for everything, yes. Anyhow. We were big time serious. And it wasn't just physical attraction either. Not on my part. Although women sometimes have been known in the past to think of me as a machine of sorts. You know. Built to please. A real boy toy. They didn't even try to get to know me, not the real me. They just used me for my more obvious physical attributes. But she was different. Don't laugh. She had a beautiful mind and recognized that in me too. We really connected.

Examples. You want examples. Well. Like we talked about everything under the sun. Like for example my shirt, this one that I'm still wearing right now. She thought it was silk, but I told her it's actually a polyester blend. They do nice things with polyester now. Here, feel it, it feels just like silk. Go ahead. Don't be shy. I don't bite. Well, innocent until proven guilty on that one, right. I mean really. Yes, I suppose that particular piece of evidence is pretty damning. But doesn't that feel nice. Doesn't it feel like silk. And my keys. She asked about my keys. Wanted to know why I had so many and if I could move them to my back pocket so she wouldn't get cut or poked.

No. Of course that's not all. I'm just giving you the examples that are fresh in my head. I asked her stuff about herself too. I understand that healthy relationships are about give and take. I didn't just fall off the cabbage truck you know. It's a fifty-fifty thing. I asked her, for example, how old she was and when she told me then right off the bat, I told her that she looked five years younger than that. See. That's how fast my mind works. Snap. Like that. Always one step ahead. And I asked what she had planned for the weekend and she told me she was going to slow cook a corn beef for her nephew's baptism on Sunday. See. That's what I'm talking about.

I must admit that the more I got to know her the more I thought that she was the one. You know what I'm trying to say. I mean we had so much in common in terms of background and goals and so forth. We were really getting to know each other. Learning those funny, quirky things about each other that nobody else knows. Like did you know that she auditioned for the Fly Girls back in whenever that was. Remember that show with the colored guys and the Fly Girls. I kidded her about that one. I sang the theme song to her, you know, that they'd play at the beginning of each show when the girls were dancing. It went like: *Everybody here is equally kind, everybody here is equally kind, everybody, everybody, everybody.* Sound familiar. Yeah. But I'm a big kidder, you know. Women value a sense of humor more than anything else. Even penis size. That's according to *Vogue*. I know, I couldn't believe it either at first, but they did a survey. What's that. No, not all the time. I just flip through it to stay up on women's issues. I file that kind of information away. My mind is like a computer in that way. That's how I operate. That's why I'm so successful with ladies, if you know what I mean. I store all that stuff away until I need it and then, Shazam, it's like I pull it out of nowhere. My mental .

Just waiting for the right moment. Like a cat waiting to pounce. It's all about timing. To me it's like Jerry Rice studying game film or Barry Bonds reading up on opposing pitchers. You follow where I'm going with this sports thing here. Because that's what it is to me. Chasing the females is a sport to me. That's why I stay in shape. I consider myself an athlete. Feel this. Go ahead. That's right. The curls are for the girls, baby. Well. Usually it's a little harder than that but I've been under the weather lately. That and they're remodeling the 24-Hour Fitness, so it's really been a couple three months. I use the one on Ocean Avenue. But you should see me when I'm in shape. I shave everything. It helps with the definition. And it's cleaner that way. Women appreciate that. I just had my scrotum waxed and I'm giving serious though to electrolysis. And I had this guy take Polaroids once and sometimes I hand them out with my business cards. Pardon. Well. That is true. I did say that because I'm actually between jobs right now and they help me maintain a certain image. Check it out, though. A girl like Mercedes isn't going to be seen around town with some scrub. You like that. I came up with that on my own. I like the way it sounds: *Your pleasure is my business*. I figure it keeps the doors open in terms of whatever career path I eventually choose to go down. Ideally you mean. Well. I want to star in adult films. Obviously.

Right. So, Mercedes could tell I worked out right away. When we first met. She was rubbing on my chest and my shoulders and my stomach. Between you and me though, I had to suck in my gut a little because I've been going easy on the abs lately. You know how it is. But I used to have the abs of truth. You could do laundry on my stomach. No, not like a washing machine, like a washboard. Are you making fun. I'm not sure I like your attitude. What is this now, good cop, funny cop. Maybe I should make that call after all. Okay. All right. Well, sure, can I get a soda pop. Caffeine-free Diet Coke. Please. Thank you. All right. I am calm. I'm calming down now. Thank you.

Is this caffeine-free. Perfect. Anyhow. Oops. What'd you shake this thing up. Jesus Christ. All right. Paper towels or something. Great. Thanks. All right. So, she was into me. That's what I'm trying to tell you. That's my point. Head over heels. What's that. No. That is not what I mean. See there you go again. She was only like five-foot-nothing so that's why I told her to keep them on. If you must know. But everything was going great. That's what I mean. It breaks my heart if you can believe that because I sure can't. I'm usually on the other end of that one, if you know what I mean. I'm not sure what I did wrong. I was trying so hard. Going that extra mile. I even wanted her to meet my mom. What. No. It's just us two. Yeah, I'm in between condos right now so I'm staying at my mom's on Joost. By Glenn Park BART. Anyhow. We had big plans for the future. Big plans. White picket fences. Puppy dogs. Hot oil. You know the drill.

I think Mercedes and Mom would've really hit it off too. Well. In some ways. But I wouldn't have been able to tell her where we first met. Not in a million years. The thing you must understand about my mom is she's old fashioned. Kind of naïve to the ways of the world, if you know what I mean. She doesn't have a handle on how things work today. The whole dating scene. She doesn't get out much. Not since she took ill. That was back in 1974. So, she's in a time warp. Stuck back in the days when, well, I don't even know what the heck they did back then. She watches a lot of television. You know, game shows, talk shows. What's that. Yeah. Probably. What time is it. I think she's watching *Wheel of Fortune* reruns. Is that absolutely necessary. Well. Go ahead then. Be my guest. She won't pick up, though. She'll think it's Regis calling. That's her thing. She never knows the answers so she's afraid to be a lifeline.

I know. But I figured this background would be important for you guys to know. I am trying to cooperate. I am trying to be helpful. Aren't I answering your questions. All right then. My point is that everything was going in a really good direction. None of that stuff that happened was any kind of premeditated or anything like that. It was a thing of passion. I was out of my mind for that girl. That's how it was. It's almost like I'm conducting my own investigation here. You know what I'm saying. It's like I'm trying to get to the bottom of this thing. Why she suddenly turned on me after all we'd been through. The ups and downs, good times, etc. So, we're in this together—me and you guys. We're on the same team here. That's how I see it. That's my point. My point is that I'm not the bad guy here. Well. That's right. I guess technically I am the bad guy here, but I want to know when things started to go sour because I don't have a clue.

Exactly. Thank you. That's my question. What is up with rules. You don't go and impose rules like that on people you care about. Not if you really care you don't. So, that's my thing. When she told me that she had two rules I just kind of lost it for a minute. No. Not right away. I mean she laid down the law as it were and I tried to go along with it, with her two golden rules. Are you married. How about you. Well then, you both know what I'm talking about. When your old lady says jump, I'm sure you say how far because you know how bad things can get if you don't. Am I right or am I right. In the doghouse, baby. The cold shoulder. Sleeping on the couch. A little Ben Gay in the recreational Vaseline jar. That tired old song-and-dance routine.

Things were going so good and I didn't want to screw it up so I went along with it for as long as I could. What. Didn't I mention that already. Sure. Sorry. I thought I told you already. Her two rules were, and this is a verbatim quote: *A) no rough stuff and B) don't touch my privates.* You think that's funny. Wait a minute. Hold up. This is no joke. You can see my dilemma. It was like a catch twenty-three or whatever that is. I had to break the first rule in order to break the second one. But see that's what I'm talking about. We were way past that stage as far as I'm concerned. You mean specifically. Because like I said before, we were really connected. It was eerie how close we got so quick. Do you believe in love at first sight. Well. Anyhow. It was like that. So, I'm not sure how important that is in terms of the ways we normally measure time. Not sure how that'll help you here in your investigation. Our investigation, really. Right. In many ways I'm the victim here. Well. No.

You're right. Not in that all-important way. That's true. What was your question again. Right.

Well. From the first time I went up to her with that one about me driving until Big Bruce and Pablo came to get me and made me sit on the curb outside on O'Farrell to wait for your guys, it was like three or four minutes. No more than five because we walked straight from the token window to the Copenhagen Room and her song hadn't even finished yet. I think it was *Rag Doll* by Bon Jovi. Yeah. That's a classic. And she was definitely daddy's little cutie, if you know what I mean. So, in terms of actual time, I knew her for a couple minutes or so. But if you've been listening to me at all you'll see that this is bigger than that and I've really known her for my whole life. Or longer. Because she was the one. But I have to tell you. Truth be told. All things considered. No regrets. Better to have loved and lost than whatever or however that goes. That was no holds barred the best three minutes of my life. Now do I need a lawyer or what.

pop song

she thinks
of a pop song
            by a boy band

when he pukes into his pillow

tells her she's a rotten whore

rotten to the core

& reaches for his smokes
~ eskimo

FALLING

I hit her and it felt good. Then the rain in Siena smelled different. Better somehow. I listened to it from our room not far from Il Campo. There was a baby crying in what looked like apartments across the dead-end alley. There were potatoes and red bell peppers frying in olive oil in the kitchen of Osteria da Divo at street level.

Elena cried and cursed me in her native tongue.

I called her a bitch in English.

Her nose was bleeding but just a little bit.

She shoved a tissue into her left nostril.

Then she got up to use the toilet in the tiny bathroom.

Elena didn't speak much English. She was a decent dancer; she grooved like she watched a lot of MTV—with all the latest moves. The door was open and I listened to her clean herself up. I wondered if she used the bidet anymore but couldn't tell from the sounds she made. My clothes were on the floor, in a pile under the desk. I was dizzy from the previous night's grappa and sticky from reckless sex. I touched myself. She returned to bed and I pretended to sleep because now I felt bad about hitting her but Jesus fucking Christ. When her breath was heavy, I opened my eyes and got up and the rain had stopped, and a jigsaw-puzzle piece of blue sky was jammed among gothic rooftop silhouettes.

Fat pigeons were battling for position on the shit-stained ledge of an adjacent building. Forgotten laundry was dripping on a line supported by a rusted pulley system one floor down: two black bras, a few colorful G-strings, some white camisoles. There was movement behind the green-shuttered window where the clothesline originated. A soft light was on. There was a transistor radio that hummed at odd intervals. I imagined the girl who wore the under garments. I imagined her small but just right and living alone. Dark skin smooth like polished wood and those eager Italian eyes and smoking an American cigarette. A university girl, perhaps. I waited for her to appear so I could smile at her. Then the cracked bell of the Torre Mangia stirred me from my state of musing.

The great horse race was about to begin.

I got dressed and left the pension quietly, following the red-brick swath of Casato di Sotto. The sky was a deep cobalt dome. I circumvented a courtyard bearing a flower-decked well and the pungent purple perfume of bougainvillea bracts reminded me of our first encounter. When everything was possible and we were still oblivious.

Oblivious to each other's abundant imperfections.

***

The first time I met Elena her fiancé was pontificating on the race, Palio di Siena. He was holding court with a group of us backpackers on a beach in Cinque Terra, in the town of Vernazza, smoking dope. He had perfect hair and he'd been to the World Cup and the Super Bowl and the NBA Finals and he said the Palio was by far the best sporting event he'd ever witnessed. He said there was so much passion. He used his hands for emphasis. He was clearly full of shit but nonetheless a good storyteller and most of the people were hanging on his every word. Elena, however, looked bored when he spoke as though he was a one-trick pony and she had long ago tired of his act.

Then she noticed me looking at her and she smiled, and it was at that precise moment I decided to take her away from him.

I didn't want his Rolex or his pinky ring or his diamond ear stud.

Not yet anyhow.

Although an unquenchable sense of yearning is typical of my condition.

Over the next few hours I watched her, she watched me. She was wearing a thin cotton skirt that was nearly transparent when the sun caught it just right and later, we were alone, and I put my hand on the inside of her thigh and it was warm. Her mouth was wet and tasting her lips and tongue was a beautiful mess like eating a ripe mango. She agreed to go to Siena with me on the train and so I then decided to steal Jerry's horse race, too.

She told him that her aging mother was sick.

Elena was clearly a practiced liar, which I immediately recognized as a by-product of most addictions.

***

And so now here I was on the morning of the Palio. Elena was asleep. I was half-tweaked and half-dressed and stumbling around outside until I fell in with a parade of young people from San Domenico. We marched about the city drinking dolce vino and screaming songs and presaging doom and damnation for the other neighborhoods because the great horse race pits them against each other; it was a wild scene. In the chapel of the Piazza riders from the ten competing contrade attended a mass delivered by the Archbishop of Siena who invoked the protection of the Madonna for man and beast.

A medieval spirit permeated the ceremony and the smell of alcohol and human sweat. In the ensuing provaccia riders tested their mounts. Then they joined their captains and various officials in the Palazzo to review contest regulations. I befriended a man named Marcello and we shared his makeshift lunch of prosciutto and melon and day-old sweet bread. Marcello cut the bread with a sharp pocketknife and the ends of his fingernails were dark and square. He had the rope-strong hands and arms of a farmer.

Either that or a chronic heroin user.

A different impression of Marcello began to form in my mind.

Images of dark alleys and dirty needles and a length of rubber tubing.

Then the soft snaps of ox hide nerbos or whips and the warning chimes of Sunto sparked the donning of traditional costumes by locals chosen for the comparsa. They eventually took their spots proudly in the historical procession while the horses were blessed. A bean-black steed flashed its gums at me and rolled its eyes and elevated its velvety tail and shit on the marble floor of the church—apparently a sign of good luck.

The crowd became restless as the chaplain, as if in invocation, exhorted each animal to maximum effort. Then with an inclusive sweeping gesture he said, Go now and return a winner. We roared as one. I could feel my heart bouncing underneath my cotton shirt, underneath my skin, against my ribs. It was like a bee trapped inside a plastic cup.

Elena's fiancé was right.

What a fucking rush.

I almost felt worse about enjoying his race than I did about corrupting his girl.

Almost.

Then I bumped a tall German tourist with a video camera, hugged a half-empty liter jug to my chest and advanced with the mass of humanity to the rhythm of random trumpets and the Palio anthem and the tower bell. We entered the Piazza from the Bucca del Casato amid waving scarves and the breeze-blown bandierino, which would ultimately be given to the day's champion. Marcello told me that the banner moved not according to the direction of the wind, but rather as a sign of which section of the city would win the race. Then he put his fingers to his lips and said, Shhhhh. Then a silence impossible for ten thousand Tuscans cloaked the formalities like a blanket. I could smell the anticipation. I could taste it and my mouth was dry, so I took a long drink.

My strong hand was shaking.

My chemicals were off balance.

I was going to need to get right soon.

Then horses and riders entered from the Cortile of the Podesta and the square was a palette of colors representing the rival factions. A local cop handsome in dress blues delivered to the presiding mossiere a sealed envelope containing the starting sequence. Marcello whispered that it was decided ahead of time who would start from the canapi and who would ride in the tenth position and sly proposals were made to entice riders to block or favor a given contrada. Jockeys carefully prodded their mounts to the rope.

For a moment I became distracted by a sense that I was shrinking.

Then a blast from the mortaretto was catalyst to a perfect fury. Horses exploded forward all muscle and mucus and manmade indignation while riders beat each other with the short whips. I was pushed and pulled by anonymous hands, and bottles and rocks and even a solitary leather shoe littered the earthen track in the angry wake. And in a cumulative display the mob vented repressed passions and employed gestures and language unthinkable under normal circumstances. Rounding San Martino several riders miscalculated the severity of both curve and descent, and they spilled along its outer edges onto mattresses placed there to protect them from serious injury. Some riderless horses continued, intuiting that crossing the finish line scosso—sans jockey—was acceptable.

Marcello put a young boy, maybe his son, on his shoulders and they both grinned at me. I drank wine from a leather sack. Several mishaps occurred at Casato, a steep and sharp uphill bend, and one unseated and bloodied jockey actually got up and grabbed the testicles of his frothy equine in an effort to inspire victory, but time was lost.

In less than a minute it was over.

But I didn't want it to be over.

I never wanted it to end.

The feeling of euphoria I'd been chasing for so long.

And now once more I was empty and alone.

The winning flag was quickly displayed from the Palazzo Publico and members of the triumphant contrada sang an incoherent version of Te Deum from the cathedral steps. Marcello removed the boy from his shoulders. Then the quieted crowd dispersed and Marcello took my hand and said, Ciao. Then they were gone. Just like fucking that.

It was a day of abrupt conclusions.

The Palio had started like nothing I ever experienced before.

Then it ended just like everything else always does.

And I was despondent.

So I closed my eyes and when I woke up I felt lost and sad and anxious because the alcohol and the sun and everything else I had done was finally catching up to me and there were some young women sitting together at an outside café. I accused them of being gypsies or hookers and they laughed. The taller one grinned and said something in her language to her friends and took me on her Vespa. We buzzed between buildings, bounced on skinny knob-cobbled streets. There was of course magic in her purse.

***

Elena was there when I returned to the pension later that night. She was watching a low-budget talent show on the television. It didn't appear as though she'd left the room or even the bed. I told her that she'd missed the Palio. I described for her what I had witnessed in detail. I was born again, brimming with enthusiasm, grasping at straws.

It was amazing, I said.

That stupid asshole race, she said.

With the taste of strange pussy still on my lips I tried to kiss her.

But she pushed me away.

It's nothing to me, she said. That race.

It hurt me to hear her say it.

Now she was taking something away from me.

Maybe all I had left in the world.

So I called her a whore.

I wanted to hit her again but this time for a different reason.

Crystal no longer ripped blissfully through my veins and once again I was falling fast from a great height. The fear of sudden impact always brought out the worst in me.

Elena recognized what was happening to me because she had seen it before.

She laughed in sudden bursts that were not unlike gunfire and told me to stop calling the kettle black. I noticed that she'd been crying too and the screen illuminated her face in a strange green light that made even her look ugly. There was an empty brown container from the farmacia on the nightstand. I picked it up and read it and turned to her.

But she wouldn't acknowledge me.

I couldn't see the meat of her eyes.

She called me a sonofabitch in a broken whisper.

I sat on a corner of the bed and beneath the sheets she jerked away from me suddenly and violently. I knew she wanted me to react somehow, but I couldn't do it anymore. It had become a tiresome dance between us. Our relationship had lasted four weeks that felt like four hundred years when we were not either fucking or completely stoned. Crashing hard and weak and unable to stay upright any longer, I put my head on a pillow and closed my eyes and tried to imagine myself as a lone black bird flying among the dusk-metal clouds and looking down at the city reposed in the twilight, stretching its legs from Il Campo, discharging a tangible sigh that signified the end of something.

flower

a petal
fell

& whispered

to our naked bodies
heavenly
in the dirt
~ eskimo

JESUS SAVES

Jefferson puts the gun to his mother's head. Puke tangled in the strands of hair that hang in her face. She doesn't seem to notice or mind either the vomit or the gun. A glass with melting ice in her lap and a half-empty bottle of Old Crow on the table. A lit cigarette hanging from her bottom lip. Her natural eyebrows have been permanently removed and replaced by painted lines that today arch upward and she had a tough time with her lipstick, made a real mess of it. Jefferson thinks she looks like a clown. And for some inexplicable reason she has taken to carrying around a tattered copy of the King James Bible and misquoting it at every given opportunity. It's on the table next to the whiskey. Jesus saves, she says to her son who could use some saving right about now.

Jefferson puts the nine back in his pants.

The apartment smells like fish. Everything always smells like fish. His father has been chasing Chinook salmon for decades, where the mouth of the Klamath River flows into the Pacific Ocean. It's always been a scrappy and unpredictable way to make a living, and the last few seasons have been real shitty because of drought conditions—low water levels and a declining snowpack. The family is struggling to make ends meet.

A window is propped open to a full orange moon. The N Judah is outside at the La Playa turnaround, screeching on copper-color rails. The old man is asleep in his chair and snoring in front of the television that flickers. His fat hands are like shovel blades resting on his gut. The Giants are playing LA. Jefferson hates the Dodgers more than anything. The volume is turned all the way down, so the set hums a little bit. Ketchup stains almost look like blood on the old man's t-shirt. Jefferson shuts the door, takes a long pull from the whiskey bottle. He grabs the cigarette from his mother and finishes it and she looks up at him and smiles. She doesn't say anything else and neither does he.

He blows smoke rings that float over her head and disappear like temporary halos. Then she starts to blubber again and Jefferson doesn't like to see his mother cry so he gives her back the bottle and she puts it to her mouth, works it like a nursing baby with a milk-swollen tit, and he can't stand to watch so he goes to his old bedroom to listen to his favorite Johnny Cash. Head hurts like hell. He needs to close his eyes and rest a minute.

Then he wakes up when his father punches him in the face, a straight jab. Jefferson absorbs a couple more shots before he manages to get to his feet. The old man laughs so hard he shits himself a little. Jefferson's nose is bleeding but it will stop before long. The old man goes to the bathroom to clean himself up and he's still laughing, and his laughter follows him like train smoke. Jefferson sits on the edge of his bed and stuffs a wad of tissue into his left nostril. His mother is sleeping on the kitchen floor in a puddle of urine. The television is in pieces, so the Giants must've lost. He gets dressed. It's just after midnight. He follows his old man out the front door. They walk to Deuce's on Taraval Street. The music is loud and the crowd is mostly tough Irish. Jefferson has been eighty-sixed in the past, but he enters the establishment without a problem and the old man orders two whiskey gingers. He knows the bartender and they talk about the salmon run for a while. The old man is pissed about the ban. About the economic ramifications.

Fuck I'm going to do, he says.

Sally Bologna caught a fifty-pound striper off the beach, the bartender says.

That lucky prick, the old man says. He shakes his head at the injustice of it all. My fucking bread and butter is in the toilet and this whop asshole is hauling in stripers.

The bartender leans on one elbow and fakes interest.

That boat cost me an arm and a leg, the old man says.

It's a thirty-four-foot Tollycraft Tri-Cabin. He bought it used a few years back when business was booming and he called it The Dream. It's still in decent enough shape and he could probably get a pretty penny for it. But imagine selling off your dream, the old man says. What that'd be like. Part of the bartender feels bad and another part of him wants the old man to shut the fuck up, so he gives him the drinks on the house.

Thanks a ton Jimmy, the old man says.

Jimmy nods his head, walks to the other end of the bar where a line is forming.

I fucking owe you one, the old man says after him but quiet enough he can't hear.

***

Jefferson's mother is worried about the blackouts because somebody called again from the hospital. He simply laughs at her, but the old man tells her shut the fuck up. He calls Jefferson their meal ticket. They're playing penny-ante poker at the kitchen table and the old man flicks cards at her head one at a time until she gets up and locks herself in the bathroom. The old man delivers his you've-got-the-gift-and-we-can'twaste-it speech for the millionth time. That he's been giving for twenty years. You're a natural-born killer, he says. No fucking conscience, he says. It's a beautiful thing, he says. Jefferson has been hearing that same goddamn speech since he was a teenage boy and his father first started taking him to local bars to fight him against grown men. But that was a long time ago. The Giants are on the radio in the background now because the television is still busted on the floor. Jefferson sometimes thinks his old man is stuck in a time warp.

Then the old man is showing the boat to a potential buyer from Martinez. He's pissed about it, keeps calling the potential buyer a fucking buzzard. Jefferson helps him start his Ford F250 because the points are corroded. He learned cars at his uncle's shop in the Dog Patch. The old man drives off with a warm six-pack in his lap, it'll be gone by the time he gets to the dock. Jefferson almost feels bad for whoever is looking at the boat. After his old man is gone his mother emerges from the toilet and staggers into the living room and Jefferson bear-hugs her and tells her it's all right. He puts her to bed even though it's the middle of the day. Pulls the curtains closed. There are prescription pills in her purse and he pops one into his mouth, slips three in his pocket for later. Borrows her lighter too, as well as the last of her smokes. And he takes whatever cash from her purse.

***

Sloop is at the turnaround. Jefferson gives him a pill. They take Muni downtown because Sloop is supposed to meet his dealer at Third and Mission. The guy is not there yet, so they sit on the steps in front of Jesus Saves. When Rix shows up, he nods at Jefferson and goes inside the little church with Sloop. Jefferson is feeling good now. It's mostly blacks but he pulls his hood tight over his head and jams his hands in his pants and they leave him alone for the most part. He sees a big dude he used to play hoops with down the Peninsula. They bullshit about this and that for a while. His name is James and he pimps skinny Asian girls with limited English and bad teeth. Then Sloop returns and they go to Walgreen's and steal stale donuts and soda pop. They ride the 38 Line so they can eat.

Sloop has to get to work at this place that his uncle owns, in the heart of the Tenderloin District on O'Farrell Street and Leavenworth. The cops call the neighborhood the wine country due to all the winos. Downstairs at Sloop's uncle's club is a regular titty bar and upstairs his crazy cousin makes pornography for some goofy website. Sloop tells Jefferson that back in the day, before the internet and iPhones came along, when you needed all sorts of equipment to make a decent dirty movie, he used to work for him as a fluffer. I got to lick their pussies and tweak their nipples and shit, he says.

For money.

Yeah, motherfucker paid me to do it.

Did you get to smash them.

Nah, they saved that for the camera, Sloop says.

Oh shit.

Niggers with cocks to their knees, Sloop says.

Sloop is one of those white guys who tries to act black but hearing that word come out of his mouth makes even Jefferson feel uncomfortable. He shakes his head.

Sloop makes a chopping motion with his hand against his knee.

You just got them primed then, Jefferson says.

Yeah, that's it, Sloop says. They called it fluffing them.

Fluffing, eh. A lost art.

Ha. No shit. Now everybody's a porn star with the camera phones.

Jefferson reaches down and adjusts himself. Damn, he says. You must've got the blue balls like a motherfucker.

But some of them would fuck me after.

After.

Yeah, after the shit was all done my cousin would let me.

For free.

They did it for my cousin on account of he was the boss.

They call his cousin Cannonball and his uncle is Marco Polo. Nothing is for sure, but most folks assume Marco is connected somehow to local organized crime. He certainly looks the part. And, of course, he doesn't do anything to discourage the rumors. He is part of a group that owns a string of gentleman's clubs in the city and his reputation as a potential mobster is good for business. Nobody hardly ever messes with his spots.

***

On Sunday morning Jefferson's mother falls asleep in her eggs at the Tennessee Grill. A lit cigarette falls from her limp hand into her cup of coffee. The old man is embarrassed. He looks around at the other diners and shakes his wife by the shoulder. Wake the fuck up, he says. She wakes up and there is yellow over-easy yolk dripping from her chin. She blots at it with a napkin but that only makes it worse. Jefferson eats a stack of pancakes and three slices of bacon. His mother looks at him, watches him devour his breakfast, and she's happy that he still has an appetite. That's something, she thinks. A sign of good health. She has painted her eyebrows in straight lines today, so she looks very serious as she uses her spoon to fish her cigarette from the cold coffee that she hasn't otherwise touched. The old man curses at her and tells Jefferson he finally sold the damn boat.

Fucking buzzard bought it, he says.

The guy from Martinez.

Yeah.

Well. Good then.

Fuck me.

The L Taraval stops out front and some people get off and others get on.

So anyhow I guess that's that, the old man says.

Jefferson nods his head. Doesn't really have an opinion on the matter. His mother manages to retrieve her cigarette from the coffee. She's very pleased, claps her hands and looks at her son and says, Yay for mommy. Holds the dripping cigarette for him to see.

That's great Ma, Jefferson says.

The old man stabs at a sausage with his fork. Now I guess I'll go on the dole like everyfuckingbody else, he says. Then he looks at his son, asks about his fucking bailout package. Jefferson says he doesn't know, his head hurts like it's being squeezed in a vice.

In the distance a foghorn is discouraging incoming ships away from the cliffs. The old man's pickup is parked on Twenty-fourth Avenue across from the police station. They stuff his mother into the cab, toss a green blanket on her and lock the doors so she can sleep it off. They go around the corner past the tennis courts to the Dragon Lounge. It used to be Fahey's; it's always been a cop bar. Beverly Hills is serving. She has a bad face and worse makeup. She's supposed to go outside to smoke but she's not keen on doing what she's told. The old man starts right in with the vodka. Jefferson likes his whiskey gingers.

The sun is shining now and the sky is blue and pink like cotton candy.

Later they walk to Grandma's Saloon for a couple games of eight ball. The old man beats a guy from Cork. Then he beats a guy from Dublin. Then he starts talking shit about the Irish Republican Army, one of many subjects that he knows absolutely nothing about, so Jefferson goes to check on his mother. She's not in the truck anymore. He looks for her in the playground and the tennis courts and the wooded area behind the public library; she likes to sleep in public spaces when she can. He can't find her. She's probably pissed because they ditched her. Then he finds her back at old Fahey's. She's smoking cigarettes with Beverly Hills and drinking white wine poured from a cardboard box under the bar.

A derelict they call Uncle Sam is hitting on her.

Jefferson tells Uncle Sam to fuck off.

My hero, his mother says when the derelict moves three stools down.

Jefferson doesn't say anything back to her.

He thinks I'm pretty, she says.

Jefferson shakes his head and laughs.

Beverly Hills laughs too until she starts coughing, then she spits into her hand and wipes it on her pants. When she's not behind the bar she cuts hair at a shop in North Beach. She's better at cutting hair than serving drinks. She cuts Jefferson's mother's hair when there's any money to spend. Beverly gives Jefferson a whiskey ginger on the house and tells him calm down. But he won't drink until Uncle Sam leaves the bar completely. Then he finishes it in one pull, tells his mother the old man is at Grandma's fucking with some IRA terrorist motherfuckers. She rolls her eyes, pokes her cigarette into the ashtray that is spilling its sooty guts all over the bar, swallows the rest of her cheap-ass wine.

He's always been so political, she says.

Jefferson laughs.

***

Jefferson's old bedroom is the exact size of a jail cell. The walls and curtains used to be white but like everything else in the house they have turned nicotine yellow. There is a mattress on the syrup-sticky hardwood floor and dirty clothes in a pile in the corner. His mother uses the coin-operated laundry on Forty-first Avenue once a month or so. It's not the closest place to wash but it's next door to State Market Liquor. A poster of a youngish Johnny Cash hangs over his bed, a thumbtack in each corner, dog-eared all around. In the picture he's sitting on a stool in a recording studio, a cigarette attached to his lip, his head tilted back and staring vacantly over the top of the camera lens, looking a little annoyed, dressed all in black and his white shoes placed a few feet off to the side, but the left shoe is actually on the right side and vice versa. Jefferson has always wondered if he did that on purpose to fuck with people. Over the years Jefferson has punched random holes in the sheetrock and they are either patched half-assed or they remain simply holes. And cancerous-looking lumps have emerged on the western-most wall, from water damage. Three strains of mushrooms and other fungi growing pink in the corner of the closet.

He hears a knock on his window. It's his young friend Lupe from the neighborhood, she has her skateboard and a bottle of the good stuff. Jefferson gets dressed, meets her outside. They sit on a concrete structure on the beach and smoke a joint and drink. Jefferson thinks of sharks. Lupe tells him her father gave her a black eye because she almost flunked out of nursing school. She shows him. It's a good shiner. He holds her hand and they listen to the gentle waves of the Pacific and a souped-up old American car that rounds the bend by the ruins of the Sutro Baths and cruises, cherry bomb pop-popping, down the Great Highway past the zoo and toward Lake Merced.

I need to get out, she says.

Out of what.

This whole thing.

She motions with her arm like to wipe away the stars and the rising pirate's moon.

This whole fucking life here, she says.

Where you going to go.

Wild lilies grow through some cracks in the concrete and Lupe pulls at them. Where can I go, she says. She tosses the weeds into the wind and they blow right back at her. Where can any of us ever really go, she says. Lupe brushes the weeds off her shirt. Jefferson finishes the bottle, tosses it over the railing and they hear it smash on a rock.

***

Lex and Tommy and Dirty Martini show up with a case of beer. Jefferson can feel a blackout coming on. Lex gives Lupe the creeps, so she leaves. Much later Jefferson is drunk and alone with Dirty Martini at the West Portal tunnel, it's a living and breathing beast asleep for the time being. It's electric and warm. It swallows revelers and regular commuters whole and shits them out deep downtown. There's a monster sometimes under Jefferson's skin and now the sky hangs purple before it creeps up over cookie-cutter rooftops. He watches Dirty Martini get on the inbound M. There's a payphone that is broken into pieces and Jefferson's hand is bleeding. He doesn't remember smashing the phone. They won't let him back inside

McCarthy's. Fuck you, he says.

But he doesn't blame them, not one single bit.

People with money are warm behind the steamed glass of the Peruvian place, eating paella and pollo con mole. They look at Jefferson. He pushes his bad face against the window. A small child laughs over his flan. Jefferson knows the busboy who comes outside and asks him to leave in a nice way. The busboy is nervous at first because he thinks Jefferson might try to fight him but instead, he apologizes to the nice families eating dinner.

Sorry, Jefferson says from the sidewalk. Lo siento.

Across the street and up a couple blocks at Portal's he lands on a stool at the bar. It's dark in there and quiet but for some fucking tech bro clown on his cell phone so Jefferson takes it from him and smashes it against his head. Another dead phone. The pussy's buddies and the bartender try to keep Jefferson until the police get there but there aren't nearly enough of them. Then he sits on a swing in the playground up the hill by the school, going back and forth. Fuck me, he thinks. Here we go again.

Jefferson is sure the cops know it's him they are looking for because not many others fit his general description. He has a few minutes according to his calculations and based on past experience. They are probably down at Portal's asking questions and taking notes and shaking their damn heads. They will do rock, paper, scissors to see who must approach him first, to gauge his mood because you never knew what to expect with him.

The thing is that he never knows either.

The chains of the structure he's on are rusty and they squeak in a way that reminds him of the western movie with Charles Bronson where he's a tired, old cowboy waiting for a train. He's just sitting there playing the harmonica and in the background a windmill is turning in a breeze, its gears need oil badly. That's all you hear, the whining of the machine; squeeeak, squeeeak, squeeeak. And when the train arrives Chuck is going to have to raise some fucking hell. That much is for sure. It's a picture about sweet revenge, Jefferson can't remember all the details, but he does remember that much.

The black and white pulls up slowly and the deer light catches Jefferson and he throws his hands up in front of his face. They're young and fast and gung-ho and on top of him before he knows it, and he resigns himself to the fact that he's done wrong again. Eventually when they all settle down it turns out that they know Nick the Cop and a sergeant calls him on Jefferson's behalf and he comes to Taraval Station. Nick is like a big brother to a lot of the wrong guys from the neighborhood. When he was coming up, he was on the other side of the law most of the time, all the local delinquents idolized him. Nick convinces the other cops to release Jefferson. Outside, he boxes his ears. Tells him he owes those shitbags a favor now. Drives him home to all the skeletons awaiting.

***

They say crazy skips a generation, Jefferson says. I say they don't know shit from Shinola. He's thinking about his mother. Tommy agrees but he's missing the point as usual and he says he can quit coke whenever he wants. He calls it the power of the mind. The girl asks Jefferson how much he's had to drink already.

All of it, he says, every last fucking drop.

She dances her three-song set and then sits in Jefferson's lap.

What's the difference between a crackhead and a tweaker, he says.

What.

It's a joke.

Okay then. What's the difference.

A crackhead will steal your wallet and bounce, and a tweaker will steal your wallet and help you look for it.

Shit, she says. That's so true.

The tattoo on her midriff says Jesus Saves.

Fuck me, Jefferson says when he sees the ink.

She asks him what. What do you mean, she says.

Nothing, he says.

But he's thinking, I've sure heard that somewhere before and he laughs.

***

The old man sells his pickup for three hundred fifty dollars to a random guy with big dreams of starting a dog walking business. The family's financial situation has gone from bad to much fucking worse, is how he describes it. The owner of the house Jefferson's parents have been renting for years takes the cash and puts it in his pocket, but he's still pissed because it isn't enough. His name is Ming Wong. He has a Szechuan restaurant in Sausalito. He tells the old man he needs to start paying rent again. It's been over a year.

They're all standing in the kitchen.

The old man turns red and appears about ready to suffer another grabber.

Jefferson's mother starts to cry and pisses herself.

Ming Wong can't believe this shit, these ignorant people he has to deal with.

He looks around at the dirty dishes and overflowing garbage that's covered with white maggots and he looks at the peeling paint and broken television and piles of clothes and towels and sheets. He looks at the fist-sized holes in the walls. He takes in the smell, which is a combination of fish and now fresh urine and otherwise unclean living conditions. He looks at Jefferson who shrugs his shoulders and laughs and shuts his eyes.

Don't look at me, he says.

The old man lets loose a string of obscenities that becomes white noise and Ming Wong leaves the building in shock. American pigs, is what he's thinking. Unbelievable.

You slant-eyed fuck, the old man says out the window.

Jefferson's mother sobs.

Will you look at this fucking place, the old man says, massaging his chest.

Jefferson looks around as if for the first time.

He should pay me for living here, the old man says.

The old man keeps talking, mostly to himself. Jefferson helps his mother to the bathroom so she can clean up. He gets her undressed and puts her in the tub that has a yellow ring around the inside of it. He inserts the plug in the drain and runs the tap until the rust-colored water turns warm. His mother sits naked and hugs her knees to her chest, exposing her worst parts to him. Long bands of snot hang like taffy from each of her nostrils. She tries to smile at her son but it's too difficult for her face to accommodate at the moment. Then the old man is in the doorway, leaning against the threshold.

Just leave her be, he says.

Jefferson does as he's told. Then the old man hits him with a sawed-off broom handle. Jefferson picks up a pipe wrench. In the garage now. It's filled with junk so you couldn't really ever fit a car in there. They hear the tub overflowing upstairs and the old man curses and goes to turn it off. Jefferson sits on a barrel.

puts his head in his hands.

***

Lupe tells Jefferson she's knocked up. She's on a cigarette break from cleaning rooms at Roberts Motel on Sloat Boulevard. They're sitting on the chrome bumper of some guest's 1973 Chevy Nova in the parking lot. Her arm is in a sling because her older brother popped a gasket when he found out. A real fucking old-school Sunset psycho, that one. Her younger brother, Joey, is different. The laid-back surfer dude. Jefferson has always liked Joey but never understood what made him tick. Jefferson asks Lupe if she knows who the father is and she starts to laugh and then she cries. It's some black guy she met at a dance club on Third and Townsend. She's always been down with the swirl. She says the guy's a real going-nowhere shitbag though. No wonder her brother went off like he did.

A Belgian tiger roars from his cage in the zoo across the boulevard. It's a sad song, long and low and lonely. Jefferson thinks about the fucking raghead idiots from San Jose who got mauled by one of the big cats after they had been pelting it with acorns, fucking with it, thinking they were safe from its fury. But it jumped a moat and scrambled over a twenty-foot wall and tracked them through the grounds, past the snack shack and the playground and the pink flamingos. It was relentless and unforgiving. Killed one of them and injured the other two. Cops had to climb trees and confuse it with flood lights and eventually a SWAT sniper put it down over by the vintage carousel.

Now the smell of coffee grinds and eggshells fills the night air. Some skinny teenage boy with blond dreadlocks suddenly emerges like a wounded spirit from the low-hanging fog and asks Jefferson and Lupe if he can bum a smoke. His t-shirt advertises Bepple's Famous Pies. Lupe taps her pack against the hood of the car until one shakes free and she extends it to him. The kid smiles at her and she looks at Jefferson, and just at that moment somebody in the motel starts playing a guitar and singing an old Irish folk song about the Troubles. *Come out ye Black and Tans, come out and fight me like a man.* Jefferson smiles at the line and closes his eyes.

punch

he loved me
like a punch in the face
& loved to
watch
me fall from grace

(promised to kill me
& pledged to
stop)
a Spanish sonnet
chop
chop chop

he cried on the stoop
with his face in the sun
a rail of coke
a loaded gun

& when he loved me
it hurt like hell
& didn't stop
soon

my tolerance for pain is
a
deep
fucking
well
~ eskimo

UNDERTOW

I just lost my job washing dishes. I don't know why I say it like that, like I can't find my car keys. The job isn't really lost. I know exactly where the job is. The job is right there where it always was on the corner of Taraval Street and Eighteenth Avenue. The simple fact of the matter is that I'm just not welcome to it anymore. Insubordination. That's what they wrote on the piece of paper they wanted me to sign. Which is crazy talk because a) I hardly even touched the guy and b) I looked it up in the dictionary. It means rebellious. What a crock. How can you rebel against something you don't even care about. I never gave two turds about scrubbing pots and pans for those guinea bastards at the Gold Mirror. It was just a job. There's no passion there. And I only took the job in the first place because my girlfriend knew the guy's daughter or something from high school back in the day. I'm no dishwasher. I'm better than that.

My girlfriend is a nurse at 850 Bryant. That's a jail. She's used to dealing with losers. She has a queen-size heart and thinks she can save everybody. I mean everybody. The bigger the loser, the more of a challenge, the more she likes it. That's why she fell in love with me. We shack up together in a part of the Sunset I call the Chinese Ghetto. It used to the Irish Ghetto, but I guess all the spuds are dying from exploding livers and the Orientals are buying everything. My girl pays the rent. I call her my Sugar Mama and she smiles. She likes it when I call her that, she laughs, which takes some of the sting out of being a freeloader. I don't have the balls to tell her I just got canned because money is a big issue with us. Not the biggest issue, though; she wants to have my baby in the worst way, but we're having some trouble in that area.

She's putting on her face and I tell her I'm going to run a few errands: pick up laundry detergent, deposit my paycheck at the Bank of America ATM, buy her soy milk. I can't drive my 1979 El Camino because of last year's drunk driving convictions, so I hop on the twenty-one-speed mountain bike she got me for Christmas. It's a nice bike, blue and silver, but I'll go out on a limb and say I've probably only ever used eight or nine of those speeds. Who needs twenty-one speeds. I ride to Big John's Corner Store for a sixer of Mickey's, a pint of Southern Comfort, and some nacho cheese-flavored Doritos, then I coast down the hill with the paper bag tucked under my arm like a football. The wind slices through me like a sharp blade while I run stop signs and race the L train to the bottom of Taraval Street, a preferred passage that always fleetingly invigorates me.

At Ocean Beach waves pile on top of waves building up to something immense, and they crash and crumble and stumble onto the sand, punch drunk from their pains. With all the clouds there is really no sky, just an extension of the Pacific Ocean's foamy tantrum. A pickup truck whizzes by behind me flapping black trash bags bungeed down over what looks to be the top layer of somebody's new yard. I smell that smell of fresh cut grass and good dark soil and it calms me down for the time being. The Doritos are stale. A fat cop on horseback sizes me up and makes a mental note to hassle me on his next pass. I suck the orange ends of my fingers and remember that yesterday was even worse with the litter and sand blowing everywhere, even in my eyes and ears. The wind is fucking heartless. The television weatherman said we'd be getting shit on all week.

I'm working on Mickey's number five when an old Filipino-looking man enters my line of vision. There's something wrong with his knee; he favors it when he walks and has a cane. Looking at him, guessing his age, I think maybe he took some shrapnel in the war, still has a chunk of it lodged in his knee, that's why the limp. I want to ask him, but don't know which war it would've been or what side he would have fought on, so I leave it alone. There might be bad feelings. I don't know anything about history or war. I forget everything I learned in high school. I'm not what you'd call book smart. Too much glue sniffing and dope smoking back in the day, I suppose. Not to mention the booze. Jesus, it was a rough start when I think of it. *Saving Private Ryan* was a good war flick, though. The one with Tom Hanks and that other famous guy. It seemed real enough.

That's a nice bike, the old man says.

He pokes it with the rubber end of his cane like he wants to make sure it's not some kind of mirage. I lean forward so he can't see my bottle of beer, so he won't think I'm a slacker with nothing better to do on a Monday morning than sit around the beach drinking beer. Even though that is the case. That is exactly what's going on here. He sits down next to me. He's wearing a baseball cap that says *I Survived the Death March*. What the fuck. I didn't even know they made caps like that. He pokes my bike again.

Where'd you get it, he says.

I tell him from some shop on Ocean Avenue, I think. The place is called Nomad Bikes maybe. He nods. He's got this one long white hair sticking out of what appears to be a mole on his cheek. The hair is like three inches long. Other than that, he's clean-shaved, so I guess he cuts around it. Must be a cultural thing. Maybe it means something tribal. Maybe in his country he's some kind of medicine man or elder statesman.

I thought maybe you got it on Stanyan, they have good bikes there, he says. That one over by Kezar Stadium. Very good bikes there. That's probably really the best place to buy bikes now. I always bought my kids' bikes at Montgomery's or at Sears when it was on Geary. You remember that. Now you must go all the way to Colma for Sears.

No, I don't remember that. I don't actually say it aloud because I want him to go away and leave me alone. He's interfering with my pity party. His breath comes out like clam dip. He catches me looking at his mole and pokes my sissy bar twice with his cane.

You know that used to be just for women, he says.

Actually, I always thought it was the other way around, that women's bikes didn't used to have sissy bars. But I don't say anything. Let him be mister know-it-all. What do I care. Maybe if I ignore him, he'll just go away. That seems to work with everything else in my life. Then I think, this guy is questioning my manhood. See, I'm famous for my temper. It's not something I can help. Once the blood pressure gets to a certain point it's simply out of my hands. The old man has touched a nerve and I give him a look so hard you couldn't cut it with an arc welder, but he's just checking out the bike and poking it with his cane. One of his eyes has that milky, glaucoma appearance. Glassy is more accurate. Like a marble. Jesus. Here I am getting ready to slug an octogenarian.

I hope he goes away soon so I can get inebriated in peace. He's getting me all worked up and I don't want to get all worked up. That's how the most recent trouble got started, too. Usually when my mind takes off in the wrong direction there's nothing I can do to get it back on track. It's like how out east they teach you to turn into the skid when you're driving in a snowstorm, even though instinct tells you to turn away from the skid. Then when it's all happening so fast and you have that split second to decide, you go with instinct even though you know deep down inside that's the wrong choice. That's my curse. I call it the family curse because my mother always said the apple didn't fall far from the tree in that regard. Apparently, my father was known for making all the wrong moves, plus he used to knock her around pretty good until she up and left him.

A fast-red Coast Guard helicopter traces the horizon. I want the old man gone but he just sits there next to me on the concrete bench with his trap shut, which is at least the second-best thing. Marshmallow-breakers stick to Ocean Beach while surfers in their sleek sea-lion suits hand-paddle out to where the Pacific rises slow like baking bread.

This is the most dangerous beach, the old man says, displaying a saw-tooth smile.

Then in a Tagalog clip he reads the sign posted on the cracked sea wall that rises above us: Please help protect shorebirds by keeping dogs on leashes at all times in this area. Although dogs are rarely able to catch shorebirds, chasing them is harmful. The physical stress of repeatedly flying to avoid dogs can affect their breeding success.

I feel certain now he is judging me.

What a load of crap anyhow. It wasn't my damn fault, what transpired. I open my last can of beer. I don't care what he thinks. I want him gone. Maybe if he knows I'm getting loaded he'll leave. I pound the beer and let out a belch the size of an old Cadillac.

He tells me Ocean Beach is the longest and most

unpredictable one in California. Miles and miles from the Cliff House to the hang gliders at Fort Funston and even more south. He says that one time four years ago he witnessed a terrible tragedy. It was in all the papers. One female and two males were killed dead out there, he says. The first man was a YMCA swim instructor. A strong swimmer. He went out and the undertow got him.

He uses his long hands to show me how undertow works, like I'm some kind of retard. One hand flat coming toward me and the other moving opposite. Something he saw on Discovery Channel maybe. It looks peaceful like Tai Chi. The waves come together like this, he says, with his hands that now make me think of playing a piano.

The thing about undertow is you can't see it coming because it's under the surface, he says. There's no way to prepare for it. It just sneaks up on you. The YMCA instructor never came back, so the wife went out to save him and she never came back too. And a boy who was just walking by and didn't even know them yet went out there to help and so then it got him. They found the bodies down by Half Moon Bay. All three bodies puffy. They swallowed water but it was the cold also. What do you call that.

Hypothermia, I say.

Yes. The hypothermia got them too. But you see the main thing of it was the undertow that they never saw. That you can't see. That gets you before you even know what hit you. Even though everything on the surface is fine. Look at the water now. Look at how calm, he says. But underneath. It's that you must know before you jump in.

I don't say anything and the old man leaves after a few more minutes of silence. He limps away, leaning on his cane, stopping every twenty-something steps to catch his breath. The sun is peeking out now and making my forehead sweat. I don't feel so good and spit some brain at my feet and gargle the rest of the Southern Comfort to kill the taste of my own puke. I can't see him anymore, he's gone, and I line up my empties in the cardboard six-pack container, tops twisted tightly, and leave them next to a trash barrel that's oozing waxy Doggie Diner wrappers onto the sidewalk. Fat black flies buzz around me like live wires and I walk to the fringe, scattering antsy sandpipers. The charcoal skeleton of a late-night bonfire smolders and smells like melting plastic toys. Fresh fog is a drugstore frappe that spills over Mount Tam and I strip down to my boxers, leaving my clothes in a neat pile. The sun is gone again. The air is cold. The water slaps at my legs and upper body as I wade deeper. My muscles tighten against March's midday frigidity.

***

Ten-foot waves crash around and then on top of me. I fight past where they break and I swim, distancing myself from the Great Highway, the puzzle of crisscrossing power lines and cookie-cutter houses that is the Sunset District, and from the ugly thing I did. The tide tugs at my shorts until I wriggle free and then I am naked, sloshing around in a cold and stormy womb, somehow retracing the terminal moments of my miscarried child. Then I tread water and stretch my legs and feel it, stronger than expected. I point myself toward where the Farallon Islands would be if I could see over the rolling, impermanent hills of the Pacific. I kick until the point of exhaustion, clearly going nowhere, gulping for air and getting saltwater. I put my head back and move my arms like a small boy making a snow angel, only hopeless. I look toward shore and a ghostly figure is standing alone among the reeds and dunes, not moving, not going for help, just watching me.

dark

his room is dark always
but for the orange tip   Marlboro   &

his white hands
the gloves of a mime

frantic clammy & cold quaking
until they find   it
clear black patch bottle
twist top
in a secret hole in the sheetrock

under dirty magazines stacked sixteen high   he
throws it to his dry smile   stuffs
it between his lips
loves it hard like that dirty blond bitch
with her mouth around his cock
Johnny Walker stings him like a million bees
then
like some hidden honey

sweetens away his life real slow   he
stretches on the couch   &
snores with his hands
in his pants
~ eskimo

TOY BOATS

Nick the Cop is walking the beat. He sees Barry Stiles first. He's been hearing things about the wet brain and general health issues, but the reality is that Barry doesn't look any worse for the wear yet. He's still fairly young and pliable, but that won't last forever. Barry walks over to him in as straight a line as possible. He won't remember what they talk about other than basketball. They both used to play outdoors at the cage in the Panhandle sometimes. There are a couple other blue uniforms standing around. They're sizing up Barry because his reputation precedes him. Then he goes to another bar that has a nice-looking crowd. Ten-dollar cover but dude lets him in for three. Barry sits down next to the server station with the little brass rail so he can prop himself up. Eventually he gets a Jack and Coke. A couple drunk girls with heavy Texas accents start dancing on the table behind him and college boys line up to watch. The girls aren't wearing much, which paired with their level of intoxication makes for a nice display. Barry really has the best seat in the house but in his current condition he can't turn around or he might fall down.

He watches from the mirror on the wall.

It gives the whole thing a surreal edge.

Then he's back at the original place dancing with a group of white chicks. They laugh at his silly gangster moves and peg him for harmless. Barry plays along to see how far it will get him. He's too old for The Triangle but it's somebody's bachelor party. Some guy he balls with at Russian Hill. Barry looks around for him and the others. One of the chicks dancing with him touches his arm and tries to say something over the music that's too loud. He watches her mouth as though he's deaf and must read lips. He stops dancing to do it so he can really concentrate without getting dizzy. Something about a birthday. Maybe it's her birthday. He mouths the words Happy Birthday and she smiles and gives him a hug. Her friends high-five. He doesn't know what they mean but it seems he's golden. He's sweaty so he sets them up with cocktails and tells them he'll be back.

Tommy is playing pool on a small stage. He's wearing his Italian wife-beater, likes to say the tomato sauce stains are authentic. He came up in North Beach. He wins ten bucks and they go to another hole in the wall, some basement bar. Tommy feels out of place and old too. Barry tells him he saw Nick the Cop and Tommy has his own opinions about that. They've had a half-dozen run-ins over the past couple years that didn't work out in his favor. That kind of thing never does. He doesn't know how to deal with authority figures. Not that Barry is any kind of saint, but he tells Tommy that Nick is all right. Then a blond with a tray comes over to where they're leaning against the wall. The tray holds what look like test tubes. They're shots of something. Barry tells her they'll drink a couple if she'll join them and she does. She has a friendly disposition and isn't afraid of them yet. Tommy gets a little too hands-on but she's a real sport about it so Barry tips her big. She's from Massachusetts, he'd picked up on the Bostonian attitude.

Tommy's phone rings. He talks on it for a minute and Barry scans the place. Jam packed. Nobody dancing. Televisions bolted in the corners and playing videos. Tommy puts his phone in his pocket and says he can score some weed if Barry wants. They meet White Mike around the corner and Barry acts casual and kicks in a few dollars for whatever the deal is. Tommy rolls a joint and they smoke it sitting on a short white fence in the dark space offered by a leafless tree that's not unlike the ones in the story of Snow White. The ones that reach out and grab you. Barry shares this observation with Tommy and he laughs his ass off. Barry tells him he's money with the white chicks and Tommy wants in on the action. That's always a problem because he doesn't know how to behave like a gentleman. There's a certain kind of woman that will fall hard for Tommy.

But he doesn't have any general appeal it seems.

Tommy grabs the birthday chick's tit. He's trying to be funny, but she doesn't see it that way and really lets him have it. Barry laughs and she gives him a piece of her mind also. The music is too loud to know exactly what she says but they get the gist. Then outside on the corner of Union Street and Fillmore the girls pile into somebody's father's black BMW and speed off probably to somebody else's mansion in Sea Cliff. It's no big deal to Barry but Tommy keeps apologizing like he has really fucked up their evening. Barry tells him not to worry about it. He tells him he wouldn't know what to do with a pretty thing like that anyhow, Buffy or whatever the fuck her name is. He needs a girl with a bit more mileage on her. Tommy laughs. Outside a handful of frat guys who look like they're on steroids give Barry and Tommy a bunch of shit. Apparently, they saw what happened and keep calling Tommy an old pervert. He always carries a knife and he brawls scrappy and mean like a cat backed in a corner. They begin to square off and it's about to get ugly when Nick the Cop shows up and he lets everybody just walk away.

***

Barry does a couple rails of coke and hits a bar called Route 101, but they won't serve him because he nearly killed a man there once, years ago. He storms out and blows past the car dealerships and the Hard Rock Café and Ruth's Chris Steak House. He breathes in Japanese car fumes and tries to hustle a couple German tourists. Then he is at the pier looking through the hurricane fence at the boats. There is a sea lion sleeping on the dock. It smells like the worst kind of garbage. Seagull shit all over everything like splattered paint. Barry sings *I shot a man in Reno ... just to watch him die* until the harbor master pokes his head out of the little padlocked shack and tells him to fuck off, threatens to call the cops. Barry laughs but quiets down. The sea lion wakes up momentarily and farts and yawns and rolls over and goes back to sleep. Brackish water from the bay is slapping against the barnacle- and tar-covered posts that support the dock. The Bay Bridge overhead stretches silver and gray to Treasure Island. In its shadow an old tug is pushing an ocean liner toward China Basin. Toy boats, just like everything else. Nothing in this town is real anymore. And then dusk fog is a curtain drawing closed around him.

climb

sometimes

I think

your walls are higher than mine

hard to imagine

mine are quite high

& I have a hard enough time with my own

&

now there are yours to climb

but

climb

I

will

~ eskimo

LITTLE DARLING

I have long-term goals that don't involve sucking cock. Polk Street smells like eucalyptus trees and ass. It's dusk and starting to rain a little and that's not good for me. I'm waiting for the drunks and the drive-throughs. There's a uniformed cop with a razor-burned neck who taps me on the shoulder with his nightstick and says, Get along Little Doggy. His partner sips hot cocoa and winks. There's a guy with a café who gives me homemade soup and bread and sometimes lets me use the bathroom if I don't stay in there too long. He doesn't ever want anything in return, not even a quick hand job. But I have to play it right and make sure there aren't many customers or that he isn't in the middle of cooking. That's his big thing. He looks up and sees me and waves me over, smiling.

Come on in, he says. Take a load off.

He calls me Kid.

Then I don't hear him because it's Fleet Week and the Blue Angels roar low overhead and everything around me shakes like a Loma Prieta aftershock. Then he serves carrot and ginger bisque and a cheddar cheese baked potato with sour cream. It's warm and will help me get through the night. And I can smell lemon ginger muffins baking in the oven—those are my fucking favorite. He shares a courtyard with a sushi place that's run by an Italian family and an Italian ice cream parlor owned by a Japanese woman; this town is full of contradictions. I sit in a corner at a plastic table that used to be white, but it seems a fine black dust has permanently settled on my part of the world. I cough for a while. Then he watches me eat and talks about his son who is apparently my age and into sports. I pretend to listen but it's mostly boring bullshit. Then he gives me the key to the bathroom that he keeps on a pink coat hanger. I use the sink to clean myself up as best I can under the circumstances. I haven't taken an actual shower in weeks.

Then he says goodbye and I leave him so I can troll.

The rain has become a red-tinted mist that makes me think I'm starring in a movie. It's pretty competitive out there, but I have the look. Some queens come out of Kimo's. They call me *girlfriend this and that* and talk more bitchy silliness on the corner of California as they wait for a green light. I ignore them and decide to stay there for a while because it has been a lucky spot for me so many times before. I'm hoping for a lonely old fag who will let me stay the night afterward and maybe I can rob him for something to pawn, some art or jewelry or an electronic gadget. It's about more than just giving them my sex, it is about getting them to like and trust me. Very often they claim to see a younger version of themselves in my face. They are so fucking pathetic and wistful and I laugh at them inside but go along with whatever they want. I'm an actor—that is how I think of myself. It isn't even my orientation, but just a money thing for me. Then the cable car pauses, full of tourists who will not look at me, afraid of what they might see, and the black driver jerks the bell and points out Swan's oysters and Greek pizza.

Then I watch an orange moon dance behind a thin curtain of fog.

Robert is a regular of mine and he pulls over in his fancy Cadillac, pushes a button that rolls his window down. He's too old to get it up and he already has the bug anyhow but he likes to give me instructions so he can at least watch. It's an easy job for the most part but he can be a real fucking tyrant and he likes to hit me too. But I get in and his car smells like a combination of Big Red chewing gum and Ben Gay rubbing ointment. He has some smooth R&B playing on the radio: Anthony Hamilton singing *Charlene.* I know some of the words but choose to hum along. He has an upscale apartment on Nob Hill and we drive there without talking, which is good because it gives me time to get into character. Then I take a shower as part of the routine. The pulsating spray of water feels nice on my shoulders. I use a bar of Irish Spring and a clear generic shampoo from Costco and the fruity body oil that he keeps on hand just for me. And there are some flannel pajamas he has laid out. We always begin with the wholesome angle and then he becomes the angry grandfather figure, which is the game he enjoys most.

He calls me Little Darling this and Little Darling that.

Everybody has a name for me it seems.

Everybody thinks they know me.

But the truth is they only see what I want them to see.

Then he's in his bedroom drinking a scotch and water. He won't let me have alcohol because he says that he doesn't want to contribute to the delinquency of a minor. That's one of his pet jokes, the whole age-thing, the fact that I'm too young for booze or even to vote for a U.S. president, but plenty old enough for his brand of corruption. He thinks that's real fucking funny. Some of the purple splotches on his face disappear with his wrinkles when he laughs at me. He doesn't approve of the junk either but I'm often useless without it, so he always hooks me up and keeps a small leather bag for the clean needles and the short rubber rope. I hear the wind outside in the alley. I peer through stained glass. There's a dog-size raccoon digging among the contents of a sideways garbage can. Robert's wearing a silk kimono that hangs loosely on his bony frame. There's a place that I will go inside my head. Robert has toys that he wants me to use on myself. He sits back and watches me squeeze the juice out on my own. It's nothing to me because I keep my eye on the prize. After a while he falls asleep and I hate him.

I fucking hate him hate him hate him.

He sleeps in his massive bed like fag royalty with shiny gold blankets that are thick and soft. His skin is so pale he glows in the dark and his hair is a crazy white mane. It would be very easy to kill him and probably days or even weeks before anybody notices that he's gone. I could take his car maybe back to Globe, Arizona to try that life again if there are any pieces left of it. I'm supposed to be a senior in high school and could maybe still graduate in June. I'd be on the local television news and everything. My old man always said I'd never amount to much but even he's never been on the television. That is my train of thought. I finish Robert's drink and chew the last ice cube and put the empty tumbler on his nightstand. I pick up a pillow and breathe into it, count to ten, put it against my cheek, so soft. Then I hold it at arm's length in both hands and kneel over him, straddling his narrow bird chest like a conquering hero. I stay there for a while, indecisive perhaps or probably relishing my new role. Then the goods kick in and I won't really remember exactly what. Except that I'm on top of the world. And that's all you ever wanted for me. Isn't it.

hair

her

hair

is long

& smells

like her my hand

is in

her hair

~ eskimo

CITY LIGHTS

Eskimo smokes a cigarette outside the bookstore. Joxer is set to meet her for a cup of coffee across the street. He's late. She's nervous. Not about meeting Joxer but because she has some poems she is going to drop off with the famous old beatnik who runs City Lights Books. She has seen him around. He is tall and white haired and vegetarian-skinny, but he moves with a certain athletic and dignified grace; scraggly bearded, blue eyed. He looks like a real fucking poet, she thinks. And she knows just what she looks like too.

Tucked under her arm is a yellow envelope with a couple dozen typed pages. She'd used the computer and printer at the library. He probably gets this kind of thing all the time. Wannabes asking for help, looking for validation, whatever. He probably has a special trash can he uses for unsolicited submissions. A double-decker tour bus goes by. A fake trolley car filled with tourists. Two fat cops on spit shined SFPD motorcycles.

Oh, what the hell, here goes nothing, she thinks. Tosses the remnants of her cigarette into the street and walks into the store. Girl behind the counter looks up and begins judging immediately so Eskimo turns on attitude. Can I see the owner, she says.

The girl snaps her gum. About what, she says.

Eskimo rolls her eyes. The girl snaps her gum. It's going to be an old-fashioned face off. I've got an appointment, Eskimo says.

He doesn't take appointments.

What the fuck is that.

Excuse me, the girl behind the counter says.

Bullshit, Eskimo says. I'll just wait for him right here then.

We don't take submissions here, the girl says.

What.

The girl indicates the envelope, snaps her gum. You got to mail that in, she says.

I said I'll wait.

Suit yourself but it could be a while. Snap.

Eskimo turns and pretends to be interested in the new hardback by Lee Child. The girl keeps watching her, elbows sharp. There are a few other people browsing, wandering the aisles. The door is propped open and you can smell exhaust fumes wafting in from outside. Then she sees Joxer is in the crosswalk, going against the light. Cars honk and drivers call his name in a sing-song way and he waves without looking up. Local fucking hero and all that. Eskimo gives the girl behind the counter a final look and then she stomps out the front door. Joxer sees her and smiles. She meets him on the corner and they hug. A garlic-breathed old Chinese woman weighted down with plastic bags from Walgreens brushes past them. Joxer notices the envelope. What you got there, he says.

That's nothing.

Is it your poems.

Nah, it's just nothing, she says.

He can tell she doesn't want to talk about whatever's eating her. And he can see she's sure rattled a bit. He drops it for the time being, but he'll pick the topic up again later. He's been pushing her to submit her work. He doesn't know shit about it, the process, but even he understands that nobody is going to read her words if she doesn't share them. He figures hit the bookstores. That seems the logical place to start anyhow.

They walk and Joxer considers holding her hand. How was your shift last night, he asks, trying to change the subject but he doesn't like that one much better.

Oh, it was all right, she says.

Good.

I made rent at least, she says.

Ah, that's good then.

And they got me doing some private party stuff this weekend, she says.

Joxer doesn't like the way that sounds. They stop walking in front of Sodini's Trattoria. Grab a couple seats on the sidewalk where a big lamp throws heat. Tourists from the fake trolley car sip warm drinks and wipe their long sleeves across runny noses.

I don't like the way that sounds, he says.

What.

The private party thing.

Well, the money is good.

But is it worth it though.

That's for me to decide right.

I mean, I know for a fact you got to do more than dance at those.

Jesus fucking Christ. How do you know that.

What.

I don't bust your balls about the thing you do.

Right.

I mean that's the plan, right.

I know, I know.

We do what we do, make enough money so we can get out

of this place.

She sounds impatient. He checks himself, leans back, puts his hands on his chest. Maybe I should go with you at least, he says.

They got Lucky driving me.

Joxer nods. Maybe he ought to speak with Marco about getting on his payroll, he figures. Keep your enemies close and all that. Lucky can maybe drive the fuck out of a limousine but if a girl ever needs real protection. Well. Shit. But he knows Marco doesn't want him hanging around. No way he's going to pay Joxer for shit except maybe to leave Eskimo alone. All right, he says. I'll butt out.

After a few moments, Eskimo puts her hand on his knee. Don't worry, she says. I'm a big girl.

That's exactly what worries me.

The waiter appears. He is a good-looking young man straight out of central casting but with an Italian accent that Eskimo would swear on a bible is phony. She orders a hot chocolate with whipped cream and Joxer gets a regular coffee, black, two sugars. Then Eskimo puts her purse and envelope on the ground beside her chair.

Were you going to show those to somebody back there, Joxer says.

Eskimo shakes her head. I don't know what I was doing back there, she says.

She closes her eyes to smell North Beach. Garlic and coffee beans and chemical fumes from the street cleaner. Leans back in her chair and the sun feels good on her face.

stains

the fluid
borders of pain
are crossed

& pillaged again

my love
goes forth in vain

your shield forbids
sustained by your past

your future disdained
& your hindsight
views bliss
as stained

hence

unarmed

my heart is slain
~ eskimo

FAT PRIEST FACE

His English was bad and he sat there looking at me with his fat priest face. My girl was there too and she was crying. Be good my crazy white boy, she had told me out in the street. Be good. But he knew why we were there and why we had to hurry. It wasn't a big deal to me, but she was freaking out because her old man and her tios and her brothers would come after me with tire irons. Let them try, I told her. And her mom was starting to catch on too. It was starting to show. It was the sixth month. But nobody talked about it or about me like if they didn't talk about the guero loco and the trouble he caused then we would just go away. Not a chance.

I told her if we had done like I had said in the first place then we could have already taken care of it. But that made her cry. And it was way too late for that now. I told her that if we were going to do this then we should go to city hall on Van Ness some afternoon. She didn't want to even talk about that. In her mind that wasn't even an option. We had to do it right by her God.

Funny how she never mentioned God when I met her at El Rio. We danced to some salsa, which wasn't really my thing. We sat in the back that was like a yard and drank cans of Tecate and sucked on limes. It was hot in the bar and I was down to my tank top and the summer fog felt good on my shoulders and she was wearing a short flower dress and her legs were smooth. We talked about her job selling sunglasses at the mall. She asked about my green tears and my hands and my rehabilitation. I told her some of the lesser things I did so she wouldn't be afraid.

She came home with me that night and just about every night after that for a month. I didn't know it then, but her parents were in Jalisco bringing money to relatives. That's why she could get away with acting like a little gitana. I don't remember any talk about God when we were stuck to each other night after night with whatever didn't end up inside her. I don't remember Him being that important in the rear seat of my T-bird or in the dirty bathroom at the 7-Eleven off Brotherhood Way. But all of a sudden he was all that mattered. We couldn't go to a doctor I knew about in Redwood City because that would go against God. She couldn't stay with me because it was a sin. If we went to city hall then it wouldn't be recognized by the church.

So the priest talked to her about me in Spanish and didn't want to look at me. Sitting at the big table in the big room of the big church I felt like the small diablo blanco her mother said I was. He nodded toward me and said a couple things and she held my hand and covered up the ink on my knuckles and said, No no no. He's not like that anymore. Then he asked me what I believed and she touched my leg where he couldn't see. We had rehearsed what to say. But he asked without looking at me, without looking in my eyes, he shuffled some papers around and I banged on the big table with the side of my hand to get him to look at me and she started to cry again. He finally dared turn toward me with his fat priest face. And I laughed.

Then out in the street now *she* wouldn't look at me. She called me chuco feo. She said, I thought you were going to be good. You said you were going to be good. It was raining. I dropped her off at her parents on Geneva Avenue and told her

I'd call her later. She didn't say anything. I watched her start to run up the cement stairs. I took a snort from the Jack Daniels from under my seat and watched her and prayed to some ugly and private god for her to fall. I looked at the image of my bad face in the car window and listened to the engine and the rain and I asked him if she could just fall down those stairs a little bit. Just a little.

purple

the girl

puts a bit of food

buttered toast
on paper

on a corner
of his mattress

& he reaches across
reachless &
smacks her in the eye

with a purple
purple spotted
hand
~ eskimo

LA PLAYA

It's that funny time of day when the sun and the moon are in the sky at once. He smokes a joint and watches some kids burn an old tire on Ocean Beach at the end of Rivera Street. It smells like rain and dark clouds accumulate over the Cliff House and wind pushes waves sideways against Seal Rock and the blind buffoons bark at everything and nothing. On the horizon, a cargo ship inches its way seaward. The Farallon Islands are a fucking mirage, twenty-six miles out. Buster thinks of sharks. He closes his eyes.

Then it is just the round white moon and the air is filled with rubber on fire. A night fog from nowhere drops hard on the Sunset District. Buster's bones get cold. He hugs himself and leans back against the concrete wall and closes his eyes again but only for a minute. He is tired. The next thing he knows somebody close is saying his name.

Buster.

There is a hand on his shoulder. He wakes up and leaves a dream for later.

Wake up.

He opens his eyes. Catrina sits in the sand next to him.

Thought you weren't supposed to smoke, she says.

I'm not supposed to do a lot of things.

His voice cracks because he hasn't used it for hours. He coughs into his hand.

I can smell it on you.

He is on probation. He is supposedly living in a halfway

house. There are rules and regulations, but he has never been much for that kind of thing. Catrina brings her knees to her chest and leans against him. She has a certain scent. He puts his nose in her hair.

Can I get a ride, she says.

Tonight, she's dancing at New Century where dancing isn't the only thing she'll do. He isn't in a position to judge. She makes good money and doesn't seem to mind the work. She doesn't complain much anyhow. Other than the occasional scumbag.

Sure.

They stand up and climb the stairs and cross the Great Highway to her apartment. They hold hands like a normal couple. There is glitter on his shoulder from the makeup she wears. He warms up his bike and she runs upstairs to get her helmet and her green duffel bag. Buster rides a 1967 Triumph that he calls Harvey. He likes to name things. He calls his sickness Jack because that's what it tastes like going down. When Catrina gets back, she seems giddy. He blows smoke and stamps his cigarette out on the pavement.

Will I see you when I'm done, she says.

He hates the losers at the halfway house, so he sneaks out most nights. If they catch him he'll have to do real time. The other option is the broken-down RV in the garage of his father's house on the corner of Judah. That's where he likes to lay his head when he can. He doesn't mind sleeping with somebody, but he prefers to wake up alone.

I don't know. Probably not.

It is a real buzz kill. She likes playing house with him. Catrina holds on tight and Buster opens up the throttle and the Korean lady upstairs makes a face out the window. After the Korean lady a few hours pass and we end up at the club.

* * *

Then the place is dimly lit and everything is a different shade of red. Catrina works the room with a dozen other girls. An older guy with bad skin and worse shoes is chewing ice cubes and standing against the wall near the soda machine, watching Ginger on center stage. Catrina sure does recognize him. He is a regular. He isn't wearing a wedding ring, but she knows it's in his pocket. She walks over and gets him to make eye contact.

Want to play, she says.

How's that work.

Catrina sighs. Everybody knows how it works. Everybody acts like they don't know. You come with me and we play, she says.

She takes his hand and leads him around the perimeter and to the stairs. They go up just as Ginger finishes her last song and some of the men applaud and others cat call. There is a curtained room labeled *Paradise* at the end of the maze-like hall.

What's your name, she says.

Tom.

That isn't always his name. He likes to change it up.

Tom. That's a nice name. Mine's Jaguar.

He makes a face.

She's always wanted to own a Jaguar. She used to bang a guy who drove a blue one with black leather that smelled like the Cubans he imported. That was before she fell hard for Buster. Catrina closes the curtain. Tom stands there and fumbles in his pockets.

So, um, how's this work, he says.

Sit down and relax, Tom.

Tom sits down but he doesn't relax. Not really. Not yet.

You been here before.

No.

He is a lying sack of shit. They all are. That's okay. She can play the game.

It works like this. I treat you real good and then you treat me real good.

She moves slow to the music that is playing downstairs and she gets closer to him. He is focused now. He puts his hands on her hips. She puts her knee in his crotch.

You a cop, Tom.

They have to ask everybody. There have been more than a few raids lately. The new DA is coming down hard on the industry. Bitch just needs to get laid.

Um no.

Okay. Sixty for the first song then twenty after that.

Jesus. Sixty.

She pushes her knee against him exactly enough. A girl has to make a living.

I know, she says. Management gets that. I don't see any of it.

She can lie, too.

Well. That seems a bit much.

You saying I ain't worth sixty, sugar.

It's not that.

What then. You scared. Don't be scared of little old me.

Catrina reaches down and takes hold of him and puts her tongue in his ear and gives a soft moan. It is her signature move. Stealing candy from a baby. She whispers.

Got to pay up front. Better you are to me, better I'll be to you.

She gives him space and he stands up and reaches in his

pocket and hands her ten twenty-dollar bills fresh from the ATM. She counts them quickly and folds them and puts them in her purse and smiles her teeth at him. She spits bubble gum into the trashcan.

Take it out for me, Tom.

Tom knows the drill. He is already undoing his fly. He takes it out and she gets on her knees and puts a rubber on him and uses her mouth until he is finished. It isn't even a sex act to her anymore. It is just a thing she does. Then she cleans him up with a moist towelette and he thanks her. He is always very polite. Not like some of these other clowns. He leaves and Catrina goes to the dressing room to freshen up as she calls it.

***

His father is dying up there. Hooked up to machines and shitting his pants constantly and basically wasting away in his bed that they can wheel around the flat. Buster sits on the edge of the table in the RV. He doesn't feel like he is drunk enough to sleep yet. Dirty dishes and fast food containers are stacked up in and around the kitchenette sink. The cat that lives in the shrubs of the empty lot adjacent mews and scratches at the garage door. Sometimes Buster will open up and toss him a French fry or two. Sometimes he puts a bowl down with milk and Jack Daniels. He thinks he sees a kindred soul in that mangy stray. He closes his eyes. He gets sick in the sink and cleans it with an old t-shirt.

Then there is a soft knock and a woman's voice.

Buster.

It's Catrina coming by after her shift. She is a good girl. He lets her in and she is high and he can smell death from the carcass of a whale that had washed up on the beach on Wednesday. Flies and gulls and the braver pipers had picked at its eyeballs and guts and a crow had stretched its yellow spleen across the sand like a banner advertising mortality. It is a sharp scent and he rubs his nose with the back of his hand. That and coffee grinds from the café. The dog bark of a Harley on La Playa. He stands in the doorway and she takes his hand and they lean on each other against the west wind.

noose

my eyes
want
what you are

  & me
  it hurts
  to be

when we are not

&
easy
to wake up

with your hand

upon my heart
~ eskimo

THE PARROT

I was drinking Jack and Cokes in the back with Pablo. Scotchie was a painter and he lived in a van with two dogs that he referred to as his kids. He knocked on the door and tried to see inside. He'd heard the music blaring even from the street. Uzo let him in. Uzo used to play rugby in New Zealand. There was bamboo everywhere. Pablo was going for an island theme in his café. He thought that would attract more customers. We were taking a break from creating paradise.

Scotchie told us they threw him out of the Ocean Avenue Club again. He could hardly stand up. He said he wanted to finish his parrot. It was a mural in the middle of the floor, about ten feet by ten feet. It was magnificent. Yellow and green and red and ocean blue. He was an artist. He painted signs and houses too but mostly he was an artist. I mixed him a vodka tonic when he went to get his brushes. Pablo turned the Hendrix down a bit and made ham sandwiches and we sat around and watched Scotchie work. He liked to have an audience. Uzo fell asleep.

Dirty Martini came by. She had a thing for me. I took her in the back and closed the curtain. We sat on Pablo's mattress and talked for a while. She was in a foul mood. She was waiting tables and she wasn't very good at it. She didn't like getting things for people. I told her that was going to be a problem in her chosen line of work. I told her that with her body she could be a stripper. She could dance at Crazy Horse or Centerfolds and make five hundred bucks a night. She didn't know if she should believe me or not, but she was already feeling better. I got her to strip for me right there even though she was nervous at first about somebody walking in. But after a while she relaxed.

***

Uzo had to take a piss so we got dressed. He said he was sorry. Dirty Martini blushed. She was so embarrassed that she left and asked me to come by her apartment later. I told her I might. She lived just around the corner. Scotchie was in rare form. He was barefoot now and the legs of his pants were rolled up like he was some kind of beach comber. He was holding a bucket of black paint over the parrot that was almost finished, tilting it so the paint was almost spilling out, telling Pablo he was going to kill it. I'm going to kill the fucking bird, he said. Pablo just laughed. Uzo dared him to do it. Scotchie looked at me like I was his last hope. He wanted somebody to tell him not to do it. He wanted somebody to tell him that his parrot was beautiful. It was beautiful. It was a perfect bird and I didn't want him to do it. The guy really had talent. I don't know why but I didn't say anything and he spilled a little bit of the black paint on the short-hooked bill. Then he lost his balance and slipped, and the bucket overturned completely. Then he was covered in black paint and his parrot was ruined. He tried to get up, but he slipped and fell again, only making it worse. He laid there like that and sobbed. Then there was something in his eyes that I hadn't seen before. A clarity. His dogs were barking in the van parked outside.

Pablo told him he was a disgrace and made him leave. He physically dragged him outside by his belt, leaving a black trail to the front door. He gave him some of the cash he owed for the tropical scenes on the walls, actually throwing the money at him, but wouldn't pay for the parrot he'd wrecked. Uzo got a mop and tried to clean it up. It wasn't totally gone. But we knew that nobody but Scotchie would be able to finish it the right way and he said he was never coming back. He'd worn out his welcome on Ocean Avenue and was going up north where he came from. He had Oregon plates on his van.

He stood outside the café and shook his fists at Pablo. He screamed at the top of his lungs and left handprints on the glass storefront. Then the cops pulled up and we hid in the back with the lights off until they had taken him away. He was maced and hog tied. They left his van there and his little fucking rat dogs were going nuts the whole time.

***

When Dirty Martini let me in, I could see where her boyfriend hit her again. She told me he was waiting for her when she got home and he could smell me on her. He told her he was going to kill me. I told her not to worry. He was just a kid like her and he always bragged about carrying a gun and running with a gang. I remembered those days. He just needed somebody to teach him a lesson. The one about keeping your hands to yourself when it comes to women. I hadn't showered in a few days, so she let me use hers and she got in there with me. We were playful with the soap and shampoo and she used my hair to give me horns like a devil. Afterward we stayed naked for a long time and watched television and smoked a little grass. Studying her pretty face in the blue light that flickered I thought about that parrot and wondered how it was possible that an old drunk like Scotchie could create something so lovely, with such vivid plumage.

choices

is it better

to

beat shit out of your

children

or

beat shit out of yourself

in front of your

children

~ eskimo

WATCH THE CLOCK STRIKE TWELVE

Joxer likes hanging at Bing's on Columbus Avenue because strippers from Larry Flynt's stop by for cocktails before and after their shifts. The bartender is a horrible drunk and maybe two steps away from being homeless, but he pours a good drink and is quick with a joke. His name is Fatty or at least that's what everybody calls him because he must weigh four bills. Joxer nurses a vodka soda that is mostly the cheapest vodka in the house. Fatty is talking but Joxer isn't listening anymore. The jukebox plays his favorite Strangers song, so he closes his eyes but then he gets dizzy. He's an inch or two away from another blackout. Then he opens his eyes and Eskimo sits down next to him. She's dancing at Little Darling's in an hour. She touches his forearm. He looks at her.

She's so fucking beautiful he gets goose bumps and feels sick to his stomach.

You going to come see me tonight, she says.

All right, yeah, maybe.

She smiles.

If that prick will let me in, he says.

Joxer doesn't like to see her at work anymore because he always gets the urge to punch somebody's lights out. Fucking scumbags in there grabbing at her tits and ass. JP the bouncer chasing her around the joint. Joxer's never been the jealous type but he can't get past it now. It's a new thing to him, this emotion. Fatty comes over and takes a couple swipes at the bar with a wet dishrag that smells like beer and mildew and the palm sweat from Fatty's hands. What you drinking there, beautiful lady, he says to Eskimo.

Eskimo looks at Joxer and Joxer looks at Fatty.

I got this, Joxer says.

Eskimo looks at Fatty.

So, whatever he's having, she says.

Fatty goes away and comes back with two identical drinks except there is a lime in hers. He remembers that she likes a wedge of lime or even lemon if he's out of limes. A couple black strippers from Larry Flynt's enter the bar from the street and try to get Joxer's attention but Eskimo gives them each a look and they back off for the time being. Then she goes into the ladies' room for a bump. When she returns her spirits are up. Sometimes she gets so fucked up before her shift at Little Darling's that she can hardly perform. But nobody seems to mind much and quite often she makes more tips in such a state. It has become that kind of a place. Joxer buys a couple more rounds and Fatty pukes buffalo stew on himself and one of the black strippers breaks the other one's nose in a dispute over the song playing on the jukebox. Then some punk gets shot dead on the corner and cops come out of the woodwork. Ballard and Barbano and Mad Dog Moran. Joxer knows most of the guys from North Station. As they wait for the coroner's van he stops to chat for a few minutes. Blood from the victim forms a dark, thick puddle of oil.

Barbano pulls the sheet back so Joxer can see the Asian kid's face. Could be anybody. There's a turf war going on in Chinatown just a few blocks away. Eskimo is getting cold from the night fog so Joxer says goodbye to the cops and walks her to

Little Darling's. JP working the door. He's a real piece of shit in Joxer's opinion. Always trying to get under people's skin. A big dude with a big mouth but no balls to back it up. Tries to shake Joxer down for the ten dollar cover. Joxer throws him a look that could cut glass.

He's with me, Eskimo says.

I don't give a fuck.

Come on JP, let's don't do this dance again, Joxer says.

Or what, JP says.

Round and round we go, Joxer says.

He considers cracking JP's face in half. It would be easy. He can picture it; bring his elbow around quick. Ten weeks ago, it would've been a done deal. But today he lets things slide. Today there's Eskimo. He looks at her and she is shivering against the mist.

A few more months and they can get the fuck out of this.

All right, brother, it's your world, Joxer says.

You're motherfucking right it is. Brother.

Joxer is trying to turn over a new leaf. That's how he thinks of it. He gives Eskimo a hug and tells her to not worry, to go ahead and break a leg. She goes inside and Joxer leans on somebody's red-zoned Lambo and smokes a cigarette and lets JP needle him with random comments. The bouncer is really puffing up like a rooster now and putting on a show for every single passerby. Joxer takes it all in. Fumes from Philly cheesesteaks on the grill next door at Buster's. The 20 Columbus hissing to a stop. Tourists from Fishermen's Wharf, homeboys from the cable car turnaround housing projects, and a mix of tech bros and suited-up downtown commuters in the crosswalk.

needle

we whispered
waiting
waiting

& we wanted

waiting
waiting

& the dining room
at the church
that night
(pink ticket night but
you had green)

was lonely

but ain't they all
when the needle comes
to call
~ eskimo

TORMENTA

He said it was a hurricane. We used candles that were in pickle jars and almost smelled like purple grapes. We used a transistor radio and the ocean was loud and white and came into the yard of the house on Paseo Viejo. The wind was a rowdy bully too. The wind whooped and knocked down trees and telephone wires and pushed white sailboats onto their sides in Chaparra Cove, it smashed them on the rocks along the beach in front of the Alhambra Bath & Football Club where the rich jovencitos went. He let me take a flashlight to bed because my nightlight that was an owl didn't work from the storm. He told me the flashlight was for emergencies. He told me my mother had a screw loose.

That's why they've got her locked up, he said. They should throw away the key. You shouldn't listen to her nonsense.

I listened to the wind. I listened to the unbreakable rain that was popcorn on my window. I listened to the ocean that sounded like gunfire. I didn't sleep for fear of it and all the rest. He didn't sleep either for his own private reasons and in the morning his eyeballs were maraschino cherries floating in grenadine and he used an iron garden rake to knock wires off the roof. The alcoholic watched from the porch. She always watched everything. She wore a blue raincoat and a blue rain hat. She had a whisky con agua in her good hand. Be careful, she said. Careful careful careful. He ignored her and slapped at the wires that were fat and patient snakes.

He didn't talk to the alcoholic because he was mad about the wind and the rain and the ocean coming into the yard. He was mad about the olive trees that were sideways in front of the house. The trees are dead, he said, God and the trees are dead.

I had a rubber coat and the alcoholic buttoned it up to my neck. The wind pushed sand and rain against me, and I could hear the sharp shards of them on my coat and feel them on my face and legs like a million chinche bites. I waved at the alcoholic who was up on the porch and she waved her bebida at me. She had her free hand on the collar of her blue raincoat and she shrugged and shivered. Then she watched him. She took a drink. Before the stroke in the basement that he called a stroke of bad luck she liked to say she loved me to death. Now all she could muster was, Love love love.

He was big and wet. He finally got the wires off the roof and said, Watch out, for Christ sakes, watch out. He put the garden rake in the shed where he kept the riding lawn mower and his tools. I followed him around, but he didn't talk to me because he cursed at the wind and the rain. Goddamn the wind, he said. Goddamn the rain.

She's filling everybody's head with shit, he said, I never touched her like that.

Then the ocean was not white anymore. It was not in the yard anymore. Pieces of sailboats were everywhere. Lobster traps were busted and misshapen. Neighbors in raincoats and gueros with surfboards stood on the cement wall like curious birds and looked up at the sky that was a black bruise from the flat part of an open hand. The waves were ominous and rolling. Seagulls floated on chunks of wood and old unhitched buoys with identification numbers burned onto them.

He smelled like gasoline and skunk cabbage and he cut the

trees in the yard with a chainsaw from the shed. He wore glasses to keep the yellow dust out of his eyes. He wore waxy plugs to keep the noise out of his ears. There was a cigarette stuck in his face where his mouth was so thin it looked like it was nothing but a rip in his flesh. I followed him. I put my fingers in my ears and slammed my eyes shut. He told me to get back. For Christ sakes get back, he said. You're just like your goddamn mother. She never heeded me either.

The chainsaw was a screaming yellow devil in his hands. My grandmother was on the porch with the tripod telescope to look at the tugboats and the tankers going into Cordoba Port and she said, Careful. Careful careful careful. He didn't pay her any mind and he cut the trees with the chainsaw and I put my fingers in my ears. She put her fingers in her ears too and she put her drink on the railing to do it. Then she finished it and shrunk specter-like into the dark doorway.

After dinner, the lights worked and the television did too.

The hurricane went up Costa del Salvaje, he said. The other cabo will get hit pretty hard. Come over here, boy.

He wasn't mad anymore and I sat in his lap. He let me hold his tall can of beer and it was cold. He drank it from a mug he ran under the tap and stored in the icebox. My grandmother looked outside toward Calle San Fernando and the beauty parlor and made a clicking noise with her tongue and said, Storm storm storm. Then they fell asleep in their chairs with the television.

My nightlight that was an owl worked again too. It was orange and it had black eyes and it leered with a black clown boca. I got under my blanket where it was dark and warm and maybe safe, but there was some sand from the storm on my sheets and it scratched me. Then he came into my room because

I heard him on the floor. And the hinges of the door squeaked like the significant sobs of summer crickets that crunched like nuts when you walked on them. Don't be afraid now boy, he said. It's nothing but a little storm. He shuddered like a busted Coke machine and put his fat face in mine, and it was so red I thought it was going to pop.

tea

the smell
made her sick
to her stomach & she
dry heaved
bags of Earl Grey &
Lemon Zinger

Orange Pekoe

two cubes of sugar

plus the Valium

& she watched
Wild, Wild West &
Gunsmoke
in black & white

until he barked her
name
in color
~ eskimo

THE SADDEST OF PLACES

Brannon drinks until he's thirsty again. He has a bottle in his pocket and he rides Muni until undercover cops bum rush him, and then he walks the Tenderloin. Judging by the sign outside he thinks it's a Japanese joint, but it turns out the original owners had gotten cute by combining the first two letters of each of their names, so Harold and Walter became HaWa. The bartender tells Brannon that he's an ex-drunk. He says that now he only does it on special occasions, getting shitfaced. He tries to give Brannon a homerun baseball from AT&T Park. It's not worth anything and Brannon isn't interested, but he handles it to humor the guy. The ex-drunk's nephew brought it in after a game because he's not even a sports fan. Brannon declines the offer to keep the ball, thanks him just the same. The ex-drunk pours a stiff drink. There's a woman crying nonstop at one end of the bar and a lonely old man at the other end talking to nobody in particular about his dead wife. Apparently, he lost her to the ocean. It's a sad fucking place, this bar called HaWa.

There are some hookers outside on the corner and business is slow and the fog is settling so they come inside to warm up. Brannon buys them a round. They know his friend Liz but haven't seen her in weeks and he wonders about that, where she got off too. He thinks about his wife and his mother. All these women in his life disappearing.

The crying woman at the end of the bar won't shut up.

He wishes *she* would fucking disappear.

Everybody else gets quiet when the hookers sit down. They smell like the streets and that's a hell of a way to make a living and Brannon tells them so. They nod in agreement and the one little black girl lifts her glass and says, Amen. They only stay maybe fifteen minutes and finish their drinks and they're all right in Brannon's book.

He tells them to be careful. Don't take any wooden nickels, he says.

The tall one with the Adam's apple looks at him and laughs.

It's going to be a long night for them.

Then the ex-drunk tells Brannon he drove out from Virginia in 1973 in a brand new Cadillac. Got a job right away slinging drinks at a new place that was a hot spot at the time, the place to be seen. He was on top of the world for several years, making good money and he had a solid reputation in the business. Then he pissed it all away. He tells Brannon it was the booze. It took control of him and he lost everything, and the rest is history. He's trying to tell Brannon something, trying to impart wisdom. A thirsty customer calls his name and he goes away, his big boiler of a belly seeming to lead him around the place. Brannon slips outside and bums a smoke off one of the hookers.

Then a homeless guy tries to sell Brannon a porno movie. It's probably stolen from Adult Video around the corner. Brannon tells him he can keep the video, but he'll buy him a drink if he wants. They sit together and he tells Brannon that San Francisco is the best place to live on the street. He explains that he isn't actually homeless, he has a place to crash anytime he wants, but he prefers life on the street. Brannon ends up buying him two or three drinks. The guy has a daughter who's in college in Portland but won't speak to him. His wife left him for his best friend. He travels up and down the west coast. Then people start looking at them funny and the homeless guys feels bad, self-conscious, so he leaves. The woman at the end of the bar is still crying and Brannon can't take it anymore, tosses an ice cube at her. He tells her to shut the fuck up. Nothing can be that bad, he says. The ex-drunk tells Brannon to leave and threatens to call the cops on him.

***

In the morning, Brannon hears maybe a 747 flying out of SFO heading west he guesses Hawaii or China. There's a foghorn too warning incoming ships away from some craggy and un-seeable disaster. They haul automobiles and sugar that his cousin Tony unloads at the docks in Crockett. And closer even still are the voices in the backyard. Mexicans and Guatemalans and Peruvians from Cesar Chavez and Twenty-fourth Street. The landlord had hired a crew to bust up an old retaining wall in the backyard and yank a few stumps out of the ground. They're cursing each other playfully in Spanish and kicking around a small blue ball soccer style. Brannon gets dressed and then he has a migraine. He sits down and rubs his temple with his thumb. It's like the Northern Lights playing out behind his eyelids. Shit, he says. Doesn't remember how he got home or where he had been the night before.

wreck

soused

snow town whiskey

blue Plymouth tastes
the tree

dizzily
rejecting
the kiss of tragedy

flesh mangled metal

jigsaw windshield
where is she

blood
sucking dashboard
you must have heard
her plea

death

beckoned sister

I hope you think of me
~ eskimo

JUNK CITY

San Francisco is Junk City, Liz Fontana says to Brannon. She used to be an office manager for a dentist and then she got hooked on heroine and had to go on the stroll full time to support the habit. She has tried the methadone clinics but that only ever lasts for a minute or two. Now she's a real mess with her discolored teeth and everything.

Brannon doesn't know how she finds work looking like that out there in the streets but she seems to do okay. She operates mostly on a corner of O'Farrell for a pimp named Napoleon. He's a little fucking guy with an attitude like his celebrated namesake and he likes to knock the girls around to keep them honest and of course that doesn't help in terms of her deteriorating physical appearance as you can imagine. But she makes the money. It's dark enough with all the busted streetlights so that pretty doesn't really factor into the equation. It's more about willing and able. It's more about availability.

She tells Brannon that she's Napoleon's bottom bitch and that means she's a top producer. That means Liz Fontana is his bread and butter. And when she gets locked up for this bust or that sting then business dips in a big way, so he hustles to get her out. Nick the Cop helps her sometimes because he knew her during better times too.

Brannon gives Liz twenty bucks just to ride around with him for a while. Get her out of the cold for a spell. They drive down toward the Ferry Building and it's all lit up for some kind of fancy tech party. He brings her a black coffee with two sugars from Mel's Diner on Van Ness. She doesn't want to talk about God or any of that other shit that some tricks try to force on her. Well then, say whatever you want on any topic you choose, Brannon says. She tells him about a John from earlier in the night. He was into receiving pain and paid her to stick sewing pins in the eye of his pecker. He kept them in a jar. They were all different sizes. She could only do two and then her stomach turned so she made just forty dollars. Another guy asked her to carve her initials in his cock with a rusty utility knife.

Holy shit, where do you find these motherfuckers, Brannon says.

Don't worry, they find me.

Brannon makes a face and shakes his head.

But there are normal ones too, she says.

She doesn't sell her body, she explains. She only does blow jobs and some kinky requests like pissing on them. They park under the freeway nearby a tent city and she ties herself off in the passenger seat to get right for the rest of her shift. Brannon watches her do it and can't imagine all the effort required to simply maintain. He's tried other things too but mostly he's just a drunk. Maybe he's just too lazy. There's a rotten smell coming up out of Liz and Brannon has a spell and he dozes off and then she wakes him up. She's unzipping his fly and she says, Come on, Papi, let's get that juice out of there. But he pushes her hands away, not because of any high horse or anything. He just isn't feeling it. They return to her spot in silence and she gets out without saying another word to him.

buckets
(in another life)

she picks up the buckets
heavy with hot water

& carries them against her
thighs

freckled & farm girlish & damn pretty
with a good shampoo
& the perfume Liz Taylor
quotes Shakespeare for

then
in the green coat she looks like
a boy
& he likes knowing
what is beneath the disguise

go feed your fucking horses
he says

under his breath
& lights his spoon

when
she starts the car
& ignores him for the very last
time
~ eskimo

NOTHING TO LOSE

I was having a bad day. Not only that but my entire life was a pile of crap. I was waiting tables at a café down in the Tenderloin District and lots of homos would come in for lunch and to sit by the window and look out at the runaway boys tricking for a buck on Polk Street. I won't say that I acted gay when I was working but I sure as hell didn't act straight, and as a result my tips were pretty good. I stashed them in a macadamia nut can in the apartment that my coke-whore-of-a-girlfriend raided at least once a week so she could fill her nose with the poison she loved more than me.

Her name was Blue Sky. That wasn't really her name, but she was doing the hippie girl of the new millennium thing (all style, no substance). When I got home, I told her she was a little bit old for that act, but she was so busy trying to get me to do some coke with her that she didn't get offended. She was chopping it up with her expired Costco card on the glass top coffee table and she kept saying: Don't you want to be a chop head. Come on and be a chop head. Chop chop. But that stuff was no good for me because I was already helpless against my racing mind and didn't need chemicals speeding up the wheels any faster. I slammed a couple Coronas and watched her snort a line up each nostril and then her face spilled gunk all over the coffee table and the floor and my shoes.

That's how we met. The shoes. She used to sell shoes at what used to be Leon's Shoe Pavilion on Bayshore Boulevard and she sold me a pair right before Thanksgiving. She didn't actually sell them to me. She gave them to me. I had smoked a fatty before going into the store so I was pretty high, and I guess she could tell because when she was supposed to have been ringing the shoes up on the cash register she was instead shoving them under her big bohemian looking dress and saying: Meet me out back behind the dumpster and if you get me baked I'll give you the shoes free. So, I met her out back and we fired up a doobie and made out for a while. She tasted like Big Red chewing gum. I left with my new shoes and the phone number for her friend in Daly City where she told me she was crashing for a while. She moved in with me a week later.

Marijuana has always been good to me. That and booze. I've tried other stuff—glue, coke, acid, speed, ecstasy, mushrooms—but give me a six pack and a fifth of Jack Daniels and some killer green and I am good to go because it slows me down and that's what I need. Maybe a couple Xanax. Because sometimes when my mind gets to going like it does, I'll just lay in bed paralyzed with my dick in my hand and staring at the ceiling and pretty soon my heart is going crazy too. And that is the absolute worst.

Blue Sky went out and I took the M to West Portal and jumped on the J to Irving and Fourth Avenue to meet The Devil out in the Sunset at this bar named Yancy's. I called him The Devil because he was always able to get me to do very bad things. We played darts and had a few pops. He'd left a message on my answering machine telling me about an exciting job opportunity. That's how he kept referring to it: exciting job opportunity. Like he was some executive recruiter or human resources representative or fucking headhunter. And if you knew The Devil or had even seen him just one time, you'd know why this was impossibly ironic. I don't think he'd ever had a legitimate job in his life. He probably didn't even have a social security number. But what he did have was lots of gold jewelry and Tommy Hilfiger clothes and a new SUV with leather interior. Go figure.

So, we were at the bar watching highlights of the Warriors getting spanked by the Lakers and it had been like three hours and he hadn't even mentioned the career opportunity yet, so I told him the suspense was killing me.

What's the exciting job opportunity yo, I said.

I only talked like that when I was with him because that's how he talked. He was a white guy who wanted to be a black guy. Like all the urban toughies in their big pants and NFL jackets and wool caps even when it's eighty degrees out. He was a couple years older than me, but he definitely had the young look going thanks to once-a-week haircuts and facial hair that took him hours to sculpt. He scored big time with the Express girls with their chunky heels and hip huggers and tattoos on the smalls of their backs.

Them cats is famous yo, he said.

Which cats.

White boys over there yo. Five at the bar.

They don't look it. Who are they.

Some band. Some white boy band.

What's their name.

I don't know their name. Don't listen to that shit yo.

What do they sing then.

Shit's on the radio. MTV. Some video on the beach I saw the other night. I think that was them. I don't know.

Then how do you know. That they're famous. Or even a band.

They were in the paper. They're local. The lead singer is that one sticking his booty out. I guess he's getting sued by some brother. Stole his lyrics or some shit.

You actually read the newspaper. No shit. Hey, look at those chicks. They're all over those guys. Those guys must get tons of pussy.

For shizzy.

Then he got to the point and told me he knew a guy who owned a trendy Vietnamese restaurant in Mill Valley. At first, I was thinking that with my experience waiting tables he'd told this guy about me and they wanted me to manage the place for him, which would be pretty cool, and I was starting to feel guilty about thinking my boy was trying to get me mixed up in some craziness. Then he explained that the Vietnamese restaurant business on the other side of the Golden Gate Bridge was booming. Computer geeks who didn't go broke when the dotcom bubble burst bought all the houses in Marin County after they'd bought up every inch of real estate in San Francisco and San Mateo. Apparently, rich folks loved using chop sticks, it gave them the feeling that they were really experiencing another culture without the hassle of really experiencing another culture. It's a safe bet they probably weren't so big on deepening that experience by living in huts or those junk boats or bathing in dioxin-filled ponds.

With the restaurant doing so well, this guy whose name was Kenny didn't have time to handle certain aspects of this side thing he had going on. Ah yes. A side thing. Here we go. The Devil explained that Kenny had a house in the hills that had been gutted and turned into a marijuana farm: temperature control, natural light, automatic hydration, the whole nine yards. And he needed somebody he could trust to pick bugs off the plants a few times a day for a thousand bucks a week while he was whipping up Crab Rangoon and Evil Jungle Prince Prawns.

All I could picture was my old man sitting in his La-Z-Boy recliner in his crummy house in Waltham, Massachusetts with a can of Budweiser getting nice and warm in his crotch, watching an episode of *Cops* on a Saturday night where they bang down an unsuspecting door in Mill Valley. Clint Eastwood-size guns drawn, shouting POLICE they drag me out of a duct-taped sleeping bag and hog tie me with plastic strips even though I'm not resisting at all. As a matter of fact, I'm completely submissive and trying to explain to this one undercover looking guy's kneecap that I know a lot of law enforcement officers and have nothing but respect and admiration for the thankless and dangerous nature of the job. That's what they call it on *NYPD Blue*. The job. He's all right, he's on the job. This is Harry, he's on the job. That kind of thing. But somebody is reading me my rights and somebody else is stepping on me and they eventually hold my face to the camera and say something like: *You can fool some of the people some of the time, but even under state-of-the-art conditions this whacked-out pothead couldn't fool the men and women of the Mill Valley Police Department.* And the thing that would really kill me is my old man wouldn't even flinch. He'd been waiting my whole life for me to fuck up in a big way and he never tired off telling me as much. He'd finish his beer and turn in early and sleep like the pope knowing that he had been right about me all along.

What you think.

The Devil snapped me out of my reverie. I told him it sounded pretty crazy.

A thousand bucks a week, he said.

I told him what I was picturing with *Cops* and my old man and all that.

You know what I'm picturing, he said. I'm picturing you laying around naked by the pool in the sun getting tan all day reading *Maxim* or whatever and then watching porn on the DVD home theater and then at night before you go to bed you pick a few bugs off dude's plants. Easy money.

I told him I didn't want him picturing me naked regardless of the context. Then the fat bartender came over and leaned his fat arms on the bar in front of us.

Last call, he said.

I ordered a couple shots of Jack. My head was spinning and I needed to slow it down. Mr. Daniels to the rescue. We went around the corner and got maple bars and chocolate milks at the twenty-four-hour donut shop. The Devil gave me a ride home in his new SUV and the leather seats were more comfortable than clouds in heaven or anything. I was still dizzy, so we smoked half a joint and he kept saying that it was time for me to step up to the plate and join the big leagues and think about my future and act like a man.

You can't wait tables forever yo, he said.

This coming from a twenty-eight-year-old dressed like an eighteen-year-old who still lived with his parents. But I told him I'd think about it and give him a buzz.

Call my cell because my roommates don't tell me shit, he said.

He forgot that I knew he lived with his parents.

***

Blue Sky thought it was a great idea, which didn't surprise me one bit. I could really support her cocaine habit with a thousand bucks a week. I told her it sounded like Kenny figured on just one person living over there. No overnight guests or anything like that.

Well, you can still keep this place then, she said.

Perfect, I said. How nice for you. And maybe I could drop a bonus check in the mail to you once a month.

That would be groovy.

She must have just scored big because she was pretty amped and didn't pick up on my sarcasm. And when the phone rang she practically hit the ceiling and talked all hush-hush in the other room that was the bathroom. My apartment had been advertised as a studio, but it was actually a glorified closet with a toilet and a two-burner stove over some Mexican knick-knack shop in the Mission District. Completely illegal, but it was home. And it was only $375 a month. Then Blue Sky said she was going out, so she stuffed a couple tissues up her nose that was bleeding double barrel. Per her relationship rules, she wouldn't tell me where she was going because that made her feel like I was suffocating her, so with hardly a word she took the Navy pea coat that I just bought from the Salvation Army and she borrowed my last twenty dollars until payday and she split.

***

I was getting free cable by splicing into the neighbor's line, so I watched some Asian gal do all sorts of unusual sexual things to this sloppy-looking guy on the Spice Channel. As usual, they didn't show any penetration. And it baffled me that they expected me to believe that this beautiful woman with implants and a Brazilian wax job and a perfect ass would bone this greasy misfit with a hairy back. It would never happen in real life. Not that I was paying much attention to the guy in the movie, but it seemed like they could have rounded up some pretty boy himbo down in Santa Ana or wherever they put those things together. That would have just made it more believable for me. Then I started thinking that maybe I'd missed my calling. I had done a little Shakespeare in junior high until Mr. Smith called me Buckwheat and threw me out of Hamlet because I wouldn't wear tights because tights were for fags. Anyhow, I rubbed one off to the Asian gal taking it in the can to some bad music and then I passed out cold on the hardwood floor.

***

I woke up feeling like shit. Not hungover. Well, that too, but just feeling like shit in general about the direction my life was taking. The Spice Channel had magically turned into CSPAN-2 as it does every day when the sun comes up. A female democrat from North Carolina was talking about the importance of treating children—even murderous children—like children and doing our best to keep them out of prison. She specifically mentioned the case of the thirteen-year-old who beat his schoolmate to death while he was practicing wrestling moves he learned from WWF guys like Stone Cold Steve Austin on pay-per-view. I read about that and it was pretty awful. The woman was right, we needed to save the children. We needed to set an example. Forget Charles Barkley. And here I was playing sugar daddy to a coke whore who wouldn't even tell me her real name. And my best friend was a smalltime pusher/mommy's boy who only liked me because spending time with me always made him feel better about his not-so-useful life.

All of a sudden it hit me that I waited tables for five bucks an hour plus tips. I suddenly realized I was a big loser. I was having some kind of an epiphany or revelation or a nervous breakdown or maybe it was a really bad hangover, so I decided it was time to take control. I pounded an open beer that wasn't my brand and it was warm and flat. Anchorsteam. It occurred to me that is wasn't Blue Sky's brand either. She favored Miller. Hmmmm. Strange beer. Oh well. Nothing surprised me anymore. I took a cold shower because I couldn't afford to pay the PG&E bill, scraped a couple roaches out of the ashtray to calm my nerves and picked the cleanest shirt out of the old laundry pile.

Today is the first day of the rest of my life, I said aloud as I shook out the wrinkles. I am reborn. I am going to turn my life around. Right now is all that matters.

I forget where I'd heard that shit, but it seemed appropriate.

I sat down at the kitchen table and cracked open a Corona and made a list of things that I had to do to get this train wreck back on track (two things my mother taught me were how to take a punch and the importance of making lists): get a job making real money, preferably something legal; help Blue Sky kick her drug habit (yeah right) or break up with her; register for classes at City College; stop hanging around with The Devil.

That should just about do it.

I stuck the note in my pocket.

First things first. Time to pound the pavement. I didn't even know where to start. I didn't have any skills or experience or education to speak of. I didn't know anybody who might know somebody who needed a guy just like me to do whatever. Luckily, it was sunny outside because Blue Sky had taken my only coat. Another plus was the Mission District was the sunbelt of San Francisco. I stood on the sidewalk and stretched and waved at the old lady who ran the knick knack/party dress/piñata shop beneath my apartment, but she didn't wave back because she was also my landlord and I owed her rent for at least two months. She left me nasty little messages in bad English and when she phoned me early in the morning or stopped me on the stairs late at night I pretended I was very patient, but that I just didn't understand what she was trying to say to me.

I know, I'm a prick, what can I say.

Her English wasn't incomprehensible, but I would get her so flustered that she'd just storm off threatening to bring her son to collect. That had been our routine off and on during the two years I lived there, and I hadn't ever met the big bad son. He probably didn't even exist. Not in this country anyways. And I suspect that her U.S. citizenship wasn't exactly on the up-and-up since she never got any official authorities like the SFPD involved. I always ended up paying her, though. Just not all of it and never on time. I'm not proud of my little game because she seemed like good people, but I was just trying to survive in the concrete jungle. And if she was truly legit then I would've been out on my ass already. So, she was probably cheating somebody too. Uncle Sam or whoever. Based on that, I considered it my patriotic duty to put the screws to her a bit. What goes around comes around.

Orange and off-white Muni buses chuffed up and down Cesar Chavez Street, stopping at every other corner or so without pulling into the designated loading and unloading areas. Riders dismounted into traffic at their own risk and impatient cabbies trying to get by bonged on their horns. I walked to the right. The yellow and green and red flesh of fresh and exotic fruits and vegetables like plantains and kiwis and mangos dripped onto the sidewalk from bushel baskets and makeshift stands. Rancheras music spilled out into the street from the jukebox in Club Tikal and I went inside to meet some people, the right kind of people. The kind with jobs. Which I know seems silly in retrospect but felt like a great idea at the time. I drank three beers and a shot of tequila and asked the bartender about any jobs.

What kind of job, he said.

I told him I wasn't too particular, just something full time with a decent salary, competitive benefits, stock options, a corner office and a secretary with a big rack. I laughed. He did not laugh. You can always tell when somebody thinks you're a shitbag. I paid for my drinks with a credit card that was way past its limit.

I knew that I needed to network in different circles in order to get the career I wanted and deserved. I had five hours before my shift at the café started. If I could get down to the financial district maybe I'd have better luck meeting the right people. I wedged myself into the next 17 bus that came along. Since I hadn't eaten anything since the three-a.m. donut with Devil, the booze went right to my head and was making me a little groggy. I tried talking to the woman next to me to stay awake, but she turned away and made a fanning motion with her hand to indicate that I reeked.

Is it the booze, I said. The body odor. My Old Spice not kicking in. Come on, lady, please tell me, I've got an important interview with Bill Gates at Microsoft.

I laughed. This was turning into a fun day. Job hunting wasn't so bad after all. I'd always read about people getting so stressed over it. She struggled with her shopping bags to put some more bodies between us. I fell asleep standing up until some old dude coughed up a lunger on my arm and I got off at the Embarcadero. It was a pretty intimidating scene. Tall guys with perfect hair in good suits that were probably Italian, but I wouldn't even know how to tell. How could I compete with these fucking guys. They'd been to college. They read the *Wall Street Journal*. They owned goddamn boats.

***

I didn't get a job, but I did lose three games of speed chess and get drunk and skip my shift at the café, and later in the day I met Blue Sky at The Last Day Saloon on Clement Street. There was a rock and roll band from Oregon called The Strangers jamming upstairs. She was in the corner on the ground floor playing darts with her trailer trash friend from South City I called Tattoo Tom who did prison time for beating up old ladies, or at least one old lady, maybe his grandmother or something. That was it. He got caught trying to cash her social security checks. He was obviously a very bright guy and loads of fun to be around. When they saw me, she squealed like a young girl not on coke or with any ulterior motives whatsoever (yeah right) and came over and hugged me and Tom pointed a blue-tailed dart at my head and gave me the hard-guy-in-the-prison-yard look. There was a wooden bowl of popcorn on the round table with a couple half-empty pints and he had some popcorn stuck in his goatee. He looked homeless. I pictured him sleeping in a refrigerator box.

According to Blue Sky, Tattoo Tom didn't like me because I was too white bread. That shows you how without a clue this guy was. To him, a redneck-reject with zero education or prospects for the future, waiting tables in a city he could not afford, was white bread. I told her Wonder Bread maybe: soft, tasteless, without substance. She didn't like the tasteless part but was spot on with the rest. He was definitely a real scumbag, but I had this unhealthy thing where I wanted everybody to like me, even scumbags. So, I nodded and waved like he was my good buddy from Thursday night yoga class while Blue Sky mumbled in my ear that it was seven bucks each to go upstairs to hear the band and would I mind fronting her and Tomas. That's what she called him, giving it that ethnic spin that was so popular back then. I reminded her that she had taken the last of my cash. So, she promised the guy at the door a blow job if he'd let us in without paying the cover. He was embarrassed for me, but he accepted her offer. That was a new low.

I accepted that Tattoo Tom was banging my girlfriend. They would leave his pus-filled condoms floating in my sometimes backed-up toilet. At least he used protection, I would tell myself before I flushed and watched the pinkish stretched-thin rubber circle the drain like an angry manmade eel and then disappear with a gurgling goodbye. I guarantee that he had at least four or five STDs. I wouldn't have been surprised if was HIV positive or already had the bug, which begs the question: if she would hump that skanky bastard then what did that say about my abilities in the sack. At least I was clean. And I watched porn for crying out loud, lots of porn. I'd logged in thousands of hours of hardcore porn time. I knew my way around a clitoris. Or at least I thought I did.

We were sitting there listening to this handsome dude from Portland singing about driving around in his 1979 Country Squire and we were drinking pints of Anchorsteam and Tattoo Tom was playing footsy with my girlfriend under the table. And she kept looking at me like she had something to say but the music was so loud she had to wait. Which was fine by me. I was sobering up and wanted to be good and drunk when the coke whore told me that I wasn't Mister Right. I wanted to be out of my fucking mind when she told me that she'd rather be bed buddies with this guy who smelled like an old shit-filled sock. I ordered another round and watched the college girls dance and point at the lead singer who had his shirt off and was playing a harmonica into the microphone.

One less thing for me to worry about, I told myself.

Let her take care of herself for once. Or let Tattoo Tom take care of her. Let her take care of him too. Fuck them both. I'd just worry about getting a job and whatever that other stuff on my list was. I dug around for the list in the front of my pants and while I was digging the band finished its set and then she dropped the bomb on me.

Tomas is interested in the job you told me about, she said.

I coughed and beer came out my nose.

What, I said.

The job, she said. Mill Valley. A grand a week. Tomas will do it. He's perfect for it. He's got experience in, um, agriculture from when he was, um, enrolled at Humboldt.

That just took the cake. I had to laugh. I explained it to them like they were little children. Dangerous little children with dilated pupils and popcorn stuck in their beards.

Listen guys, I said. The Devil told me about this thing because it's a friend of his—this guy—and I'm a friend of his. Okay. They're not advertising in the classified section of the Sunday paper or anything. This thing is for me to say yes or no to, but I can't very well extend the offer to somebody else. That's up to Kenny—the guy. See. Now Tat—um—Tom, I'm sure you're more than qualified but afraid it just won't work.

Tom was not happy with my explanation. I could tell because he grabbed my larynx. Listen you chickenshit cocksucker, you get me that fucking gig, he said.

Things were going great for me at this point. He didn't call me white bread, though. I thought for sure he'd bring that up and I was prepared to talk about the fact that I grew up on asskickings and food stamps.

Blue Sky was not happy either. I could tell because when I was massaging my throat back to its normal shape, she suggested to Tattoo Tom that maybe they should take me outside and convince me to set this thing up. I tried to laugh but my voice box wasn't back to normal yet, so I just looked at them like they were from another planet and then I coughed and gagged a bit.

Maybe they should take me outside. What the hell kind of made-for-TV movies was she watching. What a ridiculous thing to say. Then the bar girl came back without beers and she said my credit card was no good. Damn. I attempted to tell her to try again but couldn't get it out so I made a dialing-type motion with my right index finger, which was my own version of sign language, in order to ask her to try again, and the girl was pretty sharp because she figured it out right away and told me she tried three times already. This time I held my finger straight up and made puppy dog eyes and cocked my head—one more time, please. She got that one too and went away. She was a real tomato.

Then I gave Tattoo Tom and Blue Sky the same digit but with a backward raised eyebrow nod to indicate that I was going to use the bathroom, but I'd return in one minute so we could finish our conversation. They looked at me like I was nuts. They each stared at me blankly, like thick-skulled farm animals, maybe bovines. So, I stood up and held me hand to my crotch in such a way to simulate taking a piss. They nodded and grinned, appreciating the graphic display. I went to the bathroom, opened the door, but didn't go in. Instead I cut around in front of the stage and all the horny young groupies, weaved my way through the crowd and past the bar and down the back stairs.

There was a converted school bus near the door. To avoid being hassled by the roadies for slipping out that way, I pretended I was with the band too. And I helped The Strangers load their bus with amplifiers and speakers and lights and various musical instruments. It ended up that the lead singer's name was Bart and he was a good dude and he told me they had to hustle to get back up north for a two-day outdoor gig at some river. He said they could use a bit of help on the road. I had nothing to lose. Crossing the Bay Bridge less than an hour later, surrounded by laughing strangers, I watched steam-milk-foam pour over San Francisco, soothing the bitter aftertaste of that addictive drink.

bloodlet

it was a Sunday
afternoon
when her face
moved
from the pillow
to the mirror

& the running water
looked black
circled away

as her reflection
disappeared
to the closet
for a towel
she stole
from
the Motel 6 off the
freeway
in Vallejo

when
her fingers
just skeleton bones
touch me
I do
feel

~ eskimo

DON'T YOU PRAY FOR ME

Joxer wants to see Eskimo in the worse way but Broadway is brilliant neon nipples and brimming with violence. He stops at a red light and again fancies himself a modern-day cowboy. They won't let him into Little Darlings because he's such a mess. He offers the douche bag at the door a piece of his mind. He knows that Marco has given orders to keep him away from Eskimo. The fucking phony mobster wants her for himself.

Joxer circles the block and tries to cool down.

Watches somebody get stabbed in front of St. Peter and Paul.

***

Joxer doesn't understand prayer and how it's supposed to work. He's sure there are conflicting prayers and who gets to decide and how does anybody ever know. He's never tried it but there are times when he feels certain somebody has gone against him in their supplications. It's just a feeling he gets. He wants to believe that bad fortune can't possibly just rain on him again and again. It must be by design. Somebody pulling strings somewhere.

Then he opens his eyes and from where he is now you can see everything and it's clear where he wrecked the car; on the winding road near the upscale golf course in the Presidio. There is some kind of regatta in the bay. Alcatraz is surrounded by toy sail boats. The old Chevy is leaking fluids and Joxer has some road rash and his ankle is swelling up. So, he crashed the fucking car again, he realizes. Eskimo is going to be pissed. He finds a pill in his pocket and swallows it, waits for something to happen. It was packaged in plastic in foil. Then a park cop whistles, *Shave and a haircut, two bits*, and smokes a Swisher Sweet. He evaluates the scene, helps Joxer stand up and puts him in the back of a squad car until the paramedics arrive. Wears latex gloves to touch him.

The Chevy is wrapped around a tree at the elbow of a bend.

Eventually an SFFD ambulance shows up.

Oh shit, you got real banged up here, the first paramedic says. Were you wearing a seat belt.

He doesn't know, the cop says.

The paramedic thinks all the injuries are from the accident and Joxer doesn't bother telling him about the scrap. Not with the park cop right there. He sits on the collapsible gurney and they use strips of gauze and ointment and medical tape. After they patch him up a bit, city cops arrest him for driving drunk. It's better that way, because if SFPD processes him it's not a federal offense.

You're lucky you didn't hurt nobody or worse, the city cop says.

Joxer laughs. Tells him he's friends with Nick Balistreri, hoping for a bailout.

You should've called him for a ride if he's your friend, the city cop says.

Joxer closes his eyes.

Because he can't help you now.

Joxer can feel his luck running out like a slow leak.

***

At 850 Bryant the city cop hands him over to an asshole sheriff for booking. Fingerprints, mug shot, put all your valuables in this envelope please (California driver's license, forty bucks in cash, ATM card) remove your shoes so you don't hang yourself with the laces; as if. Now sit here in this cage with the other animals for ten or twelve hours while we fucking ignore you. And if you've got to take a shit there's a dirty hole in the floor in the corner. A Latin guy is sleeping on the bench using the one roll of toilet paper as a pillow. A fat tech bro in a small track suit, sitting with his head in his hands. A payphone on the wall. The first call is free but after that you need a calling card number. And you can't connect to a cell phone, only land lines. Joxer figures he'd better call Eskimo real quick.

Probably wake her, but oh well.

He picks up the handset and wipes it on the bottom of his t-shirt, smudging the greasy ear and fingerprints at best. Fucking disgusting, he thinks. Probably get scabies from some homeless piece of shit. He wedges it between his shoulder and the side of his face, punches in the numbers, clears his throat.

After three rings he hears Eskimo's voice on the other end.

Hey baby, he says.

She yawns. Where you at, she says.

He pauses. 850, he says.

She doesn't say anything at first. But he can read her mind; here we go again.

What happened, she says.

Everything's all right.

Was it a fight.

Nah. Riding around.

Did you tell them about your head.

Nah, it doesn't matter.

I'll come get you. She sounds pissed.

All right, but it'll be a while, he says.

What about our deal, she says. Our plan.

I know, I know.

You fucking promised, Joxer.

I know.

All right.

Click. She disconnects.

Joxer bangs the phone back into its cradle. Three times. Bang. Bang. Bang. The tech bro laughs. The Latino wakes up. Fuck dude, the Latin guy says.

It was his wife, the tech bro says. She's pissed he's in here.

Joxer shakes his head at the thought of being a husband to Eskimo or anybody.

The Latin guy goes back to sleep and starts snoring instantly. The tech bro is a talker. He was picked up on a warrant for some shit down in LA. Domestic violence of one kind or another. His name is Gordon. Joxer can't get him to stop flapping his lips. Then after a while another asshole sheriff opens the door and a big homeboy probably from Oakland walks in all decked out in vintage Golden State Warriors gear and a big gold necklace and one of those gold grills on his front teeth. He's followed by four or five other dudes, none of them together, a real mixed bag of violations it seems. At first, everybody tacitly establishes who will sit where, looking for a familiar face in the cell. You can always tell the ones who have been through the system before, the way they try to blend in. And the fresh meat looks overwhelmed and avoids eye contact and tries to remember how to behave based on prison scenes from the movies or television.

Joxer gets a kick out of the dynamics.

The big homeboy paces back and forth like a lion.

Do the phone work, he says to Joxer.

Worked for me all right a minute ago, Joxer says

Homey picks up the handset and listens for a dial tone. Puts it back down.

Fucking shit broke, he says.

Giving up easy, Joxer thinks. Probably can't read the instructions taped on the wall. The big homeboy starts pacing back and forth again. Then the door opens and three more white guys came in with peanut butter sandwiches and apples and cookies in plastic bags. It's standing room only now. Before the asshole sheriff can close the door all the way the homeboy approaches him. Hey man, that's nice, but can't a black folk get some food, he says. The sheriff opens the door all the way. What, he says.

Can't a black folk get some food in here.

That's a stupid question, the sheriff says. Please be patient.

All right, but hey man, and can I get some paper up in here, he says. He points to his backside. So, I can do my business, you know.

The sheriff indicates the roll of toilet paper under the sleeping Latin guy's head. The big homeboy acknowledges it but makes a face and then smiles.

Nah man, his head been on that one all night, he says.

The sheriff puts his thumbs in his belt. Are you saying your ass is cleaner than his head, he says.

Homey laughs and shrugs his linebacker shoulders.

All right, I'll see what I can do, the sheriff says.

He closes the door. Big homeboy walks around some more and stops in the middle of the cage. Regards his cellmates carefully, looking from one to the other, scratching his chin, thinking. I guess Trump really did fuck up that economy, he says.

This guy is classic, Joxer thinks. A born entertainer, class clown.

Everybody's quiet, waiting for him to finish his thought, for the punch line. There's more white folk in here than color folk, he says. Ain't never seen that shit before.

Joxer looks around and it's true.

How about that.

Everybody laughs and Joxer notices that the mood relaxes somewhat afterward. One of the new white guys even breaks his sandwich in half and hands the slightly larger piece over to the big homeboy. Yeah, I saw that movie too, Joxer thinks. Make friends with the biggest, most dialed-in guy so he'll protect you and take you under his wing. But the flipside is if you're going to be locked up together in an actual prison for a stretch, he might just make you his bitch and when the lights go off, it's cherry-picking time.

Joxer settles in near the reinforced window facing the narrow hall and the nurse's station and some other cubicles. The blonde woman in blue scrubs is pretty. She's fooling with her computer, looking at the screen, reading whatever is there. Three dark skinned brothers in matching orange jump suits shuffle past. A veteran sheriff is teaching a recruit how to be a true asshole, showing him the asshole ropes. Taking him around the floor, pulling random sheets and discussing the details, from time to time warning Joxer and the other the two-legged zoo animals away from the windows and doors. Laughing. Talking some amount of shit. Joxer shakes his head. Eventually he falls asleep sitting up against the wall and he doesn't even dream because who could dream in a place like this.

road

winter

like a rabid bitch

gnaws my naked hands

thrashing
through swashbuckling
snow two-legged
contraband

searching
for immunity
against unfaithful land

wishing
for refraining from
defenses so long
manned

knowing

that the junky road
forever veers
unplanned

crying
as I realize
alone here I must stand
~ eskimo

CAPP STREET REUNION

It's Capp Street and she's standing dark under the 101 overpass. She sticks her head through the window and puts her hand between my legs. I ask her how much. She tells me and then she gets in. We pull around the corner to a spot she likes. She looks vaguely familiar, but I don't say anything. She puts the condom on me with her mouth. Then after a few minutes she says, Baby you got to hurry, I got to get back out there on that stroll. I tell her not to worry about finishing me and she is relieved. She wipes her slobber off and puts everything—the money, the limp rubber, the soiled tissues—in her little black purse. Her name is Candy and she recognizes me from high school. We had Spanish together and she had a crush on me, and I never gave her the time of day. She laughs and says, Boy the tables turned now. I laugh too and she gets out. She says, Baby you shouldn't drive in that condition. I smile and ease away from the curb. I smell her even ten blocks away. Cigarettes and sweat and dirty feet. Then I get sick some more in the Office Depot parking lot and with an old newspaper I clean what ends up on me. I try to picture the girl she used to be and I cannot. It is difficult enough to remember what I was like back then.

flesh

sharpened
the end of a wire coat
hanger

& carved my future
into
my fickle flesh
trade

it has bought me so
much
junk

& at the same time
exacted a toll
on
my woman girl
soul

that cum smudged
brass
pole
~ eskimo

SMALL DEATHS

I want to taste your lips. That's what she says to me. Rain outside sounds like rocks and I'm a good two days into a real shitface and her husband is upstairs with a skinny Russian girl and a spoonful of methamphetamine. There's a fight on the big-screen television. Cornfed Callahan is punching the hell out of some Samoan-born kid from New Zealand. Then he goes back to dancing away and letting the kid chase him around the ring with haymakers. Peppering him with left jabs and right leads. Frustrating him with a three-inch reach advantage. It's the second round. I pop my last Xanax and text my supplier.

Marie goes to the fridge to get me a beer. We've been secretly fucking off and on for a year or so. She actually carried my baby until June when she started to show and then she hired some doctor down the Peninsula to spoon it out of her. It rattled me even though I understand her reservations. Her fears are legitimate; I'm not really a long-haul guy and wouldn't make much of a husband or father. So, since then we've been on ice.

Not like the old days, Irish Pat says to me.

I snap out of it. He's talking about the fight.

These clowns couldn't hang back in the day, he says.

Yeah, I say, big men used to go head to head.

Ali and Frazier, George Foreman, all the great ones, he says.

It's true. Irish Pat would know. He fought Roberto Duran in the Civic Auditorium. He pounded Wilfredo Benitez in Tucson,

Arizona. He went after a championship belt in Tokyo. But that was a long time ago. Any purse money he won went straight up his nose.

This makes me sick to my stomach, he says.

He sneezes and spits blood into an ashtray.

Then we polish off what's left of the Old Crow. Cop sirens wail and the old horn of a fire engine flares up and gets smaller until the rain is the only thing again. Old cars crawl along Taraval Street with bat-eye brake lights blinking. Then thunder like an empty dumpster dropped into a deserted parking lot. I like that she wants to taste my lips. I know she means it.

She returns with a cold one and takes a sip of foam before handing it over.

I had a dream about making love with you again.

That's what I say to her.

It's not even true. But she believes me and likes that I had that dream.

This is the game we play.

***

Then we go to a hotel near Ocean Beach. The one where that singer from LA overdosed. Eventually the night manager knocks on the door and asks us to quiet down. He says it sounds like wild horses. Marie and I have a good laugh over that one and then we start in on each other again.

Did you feel that, she finally says.

Yes.

It's another lie. I didn't feel anything at all. I never feel anything anymore; it's a blessing and a curse. I move across the bed and pretend that I'm satisfied, try to quietly take care of it myself.

She cries.

Look at me, she says.

She speaks with a French accent that is exaggerated when she's overcome with emotion.

I look at her.

Why are you crying, I say.

Because it was beautiful.

I know she means it and after a while she sleeps and I slip out.

I drive drunk and the streets of the Tenderloin District are black as cats. Early bird transvestite hookers wave. The puzzle of unlit alleys smells like ass. The curb rises up and punctures the rusted underbelly of my El Camino. So I park there. A yellow cab almost runs me down. A bouncer turns me away with the unconditional shove reserved for unwelcome people. Then I make it to the bar in the next place without even catching the name. Maybe on the corner of Leavenworth. I sit on a stool next to a guy who looks like Willie Nelson. He tells me to stop eyeballing him. I tell him to fuck off. A shot of Bushmill chases a pint of Guinness chases a Jack and Coke. I say a few choice things to the Redheaded Stranger beside me and the prick pouring drinks says he's heard enough out of me. Then I'm outside where the rain is gone but the fog is a familiar old blanket.

***

Up the street now, some Chinese dude buzzes me in and looks me up and down, trying to figure out if I'm a cop of some kind. The girl says words to the man in Chinese and he disappears and she says, Okay. She tells me what we can do and how much it will cost. She has a pretty face but teeth like corn nuts.

Her name is Ruby.

Back there, I say.

No no never back there.

Fine.

Okay you pay now.

I give her three twenties. She leaves and comes back with change, takes me to a room. You get in tub, she says.

I take off my clothes and get in the tub that has a dirt ring around it.

I wash you good, she says.

Dark water swirls in circles. She washes me good and then dries me with a damp towel kept on a metal hook. Then after a while she becomes angry because she cannot finish me. And because her jaw has popped out of place; occupational hazard I suppose. She fixes it herself, both hands strategically placed under her chin so that her palms connect to form the bottom of a *V*.

You drink too many beer, she says.

Yeah I had a couple.

Not my fault, no refund.

I tell her maybe we should try that other thing.

You pay two hundred for that, she says.

I ask her if a credit card is okay because I don't want to use all my cash. And I have in my possession some stolen plastic.

Credit card okay, Ruby says.

She hands me the towel to wrap around my waist and takes me down the hall where a couple other girls are lounging on a couch watching Channel 2, which is showing highlights from the fight. Cornfed dodges Tua's rushes like a toreador and scores points with a jab and occasional combinations. The crowd at Mandalay Bay boos. I can imagine Irish Pat's disgust.

The girls look bored. They look up at me bored.

Ruby runs my card. I sign something.

She speaks in Chinese, the bored girls laugh.

I told them you big one, she says.

More laughter.

They jealous, she says.

We return to the room. She uses a silver kitchen timer from Walgreen's, it's shaped like a miniature tea kettle. I watch myself in the mirror. She watches the clock. Then she gets really mad and throws a fit because I'm still not even close and she's getting tired, worn out.

I tell her not to fucking worry about it. Relax, I say, thinking about my depleted supply of Xanax. How soon it will be difficult for me to relax.

Something wrong with you, she says.

Yeah all right.

Not my fault, she says.

I know.

No refund, she says.

Can I try back there.

No no never back there, she says.

All right.

You want other girl, she says.

Sure what the hell.

She slips off me and grabs her clothes from the floor.

One of the bored girls from the couch comes in after a few minutes.

You pay two hundred, she says right off the bat.

I already paid.

More for me, she says.

I give her the credit card. What do I care.

Follow me, she says.

The first girl is on the couch chewing a drumstick from Tommy's Joynt. She giggles. You take care my big one, she says.

Then they speak to each other in Chinese.

And here's the thing: I'm being set up and I know it and I don't even fucking care.

You too big for Ruby, the new girl says.

She runs the credit card. She doesn't even tell me her phony-ass name.

You make her tired, she says.

I sign something, a slip of paper.

Now she jealous, she says.

She holds my hand back to the room and closes the door with her tiny foot. It occurs to me that she is barely an adult, which shouldn't surprise me as I had spent some time with the awfully young Asian whores when I was stationed in the Philippines—before the Marines kicked me out for good. Dishonorable discharge. Jesus Christ. A rare moment of clarity: It seems I have come full circle. And I can't fucking do this anymore.

You get in tub, the new girl says.

I get in the tub, however reluctantly now.

I wash you good, she says.

She washes me good.

I take good care you, she says.

Silver stretch marks around her belly and small breasts, rippling out and down from her hips. I run my finger along the white lines that could signify childbirth. Then I close my eyes tight and when I open them she's long gone and a couple skinny-muscled young guys with dragon tattoos come in and start to work me over with wooden clubs. Back in the day I would've given them a run for their money but not anymore; I've gone soft in my old age. Neither one of them speaks a word of English. I simply curl up in the tub and wait for them to stop. Then they put me out in the street with my clothes in my hand and I get dressed. I get sick on myself. I want to catch a taxi or the N Judah but my cash and that credit card are missing. Then an old black dude tries to bum a smoke off me and I rabbit-ear my pants pockets and he laughs at my predicament.

Irish Pat picks me up on Van Ness and Pine in his cherry 1973 Cougar.

You look like shit on a biscuit, he says.

The top is down and the red interior smells like Armor All and cheap cigars.

Seriously. You look like you went a couple rounds with the champ, he says.

I tell him about getting rolled by the Jackson Street Boys.

He knows all about that kind of thing and doesn't offer any sympathy. He tells me Cornfed won a unanimous decision and managed to keep his facial features intact. He threw 674 punches, 300 of which found their target. Tua on the other hand couldn't get his left hook to land flush, connecting with only 110 of 413 punches. All three judges had Cornfed winning by at least six points. Irish Pat says it was a good decision but a dogshit fight. He says there was some drama at his party because E couldn't find his wife. Pat gives me one of his looks because of course he knows for a fact I've been banging Marie behind E's back. I picture her alone in that hotel room. She always worries that if E discovers our affair then he'll kill her or me or both of us. Fuck that guy, but he does have nuts enough for it. He helps run guns for the local chapter of a well known bike club.

Then Irish Pat fiddles with the radio dial until he finds something he likes: Neil Young singing *Old Man*. He drums the dashboard with his knuckles. *Old man, take a look at my life.* In between songs the deejay says they had to rush Tua to the emergency after he got woozy in the locker room. There was blood in his brain. The doctors did what they could, worked on him for an hour or so, but he died in the hospital. The deejay refers to it as a small death in light of all that's going on in the world. He's talking about Black Lives Matter. Terrorism. School shootings. The Gaza Strip. Hurricanes, floods, disease.

Holy fucking shit, Irish Pat says.

Small death my ass, I say.

Cornfed is fucked.

That kind of shit can ruin a fighter.

Pat thumbs the power button on the radio and we ride in silence.

And I think about all the small deaths that have in fact ruined me.

***

We make an illegal left and take Pine to Gough to Grove and turn right. It's a dark night and too cold to have the top down. San Francisco chill soaks my bones. Irish Pat hits the gas and the 351 Cleveland grumbles to life so we can take the upcoming grade. My head snaps back against the vinyl seat and between restored Victorians and low-income apartment buildings and serpent-like power lines, the sky is low and black and empty.

Jon Boilard was born and raised in small towns in Western Massachusetts. Today he lives and writes in Northern California. His debut short story collection, SETTRIGHT ROAD (Dzanc Books/2017), was preceded by two novels, THE CASTAWAY LOUNGE (Dzanc Books/2015) and A RIVER CLOSELY WATCHED (MacAdam Cage/2013), which was a finalist for the Northern California Book Award the following year. Jon's award-winning short stories have appeared in some of the finest literary journals in the United States, Canada, Europe and Asia. He has participated in the Cork International Short Story Festival in Cork, Ireland, the Wroclaw Short Story Festival in Wroclaw, Poland, and LitQuake in San Francisco, California.

PGIL2020USA

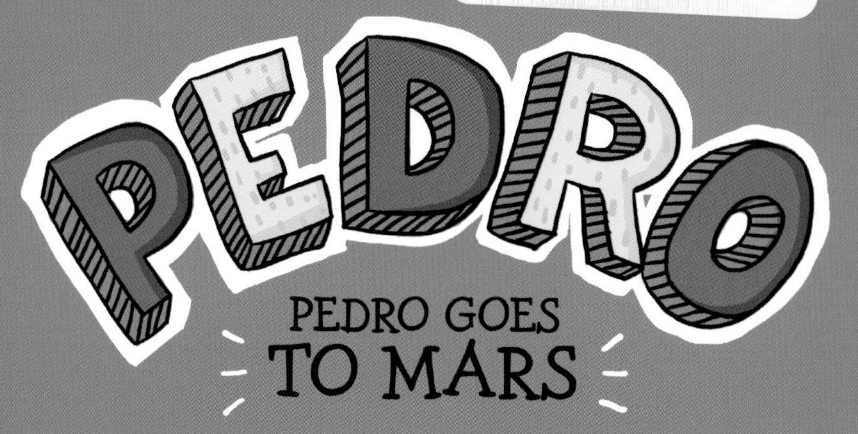

PEDRO GOES TO MARS

by Fran Manushkin

illustrated by
Tammie Lyon

PICTURE WINDOW BOOKS
a capstone imprint

Pedro is published by Picture Window Books,
an imprint of Capstone.
1710 Roe Crest Drive
North Mankato, Minnesota 56003
www.capstonepub.com

Library of Congress Cataloging-in-Publication Data is available
on the Library of Congress website.
ISBN: 978-1-5158-7081-4 (library binding)
ISBN: 978-1-5158-7315-0 (paperback)
ISBN: 978-1-5158-7083-8 (eBook PDF)

Summary: Pedro would love to take a trip to planet Mars! Are his climbing skills good enough for the planet's rocky surface? Can he pack enough sandwiches to keep himself fed? Will Pedro's big imagination lead him to Mars, or will he decide that Earth is the planet for him?

Designer: Bobbie Nuytten
Design Elements by Shutterstock

Printed and bound in the United States.
PA117

Table of Contents

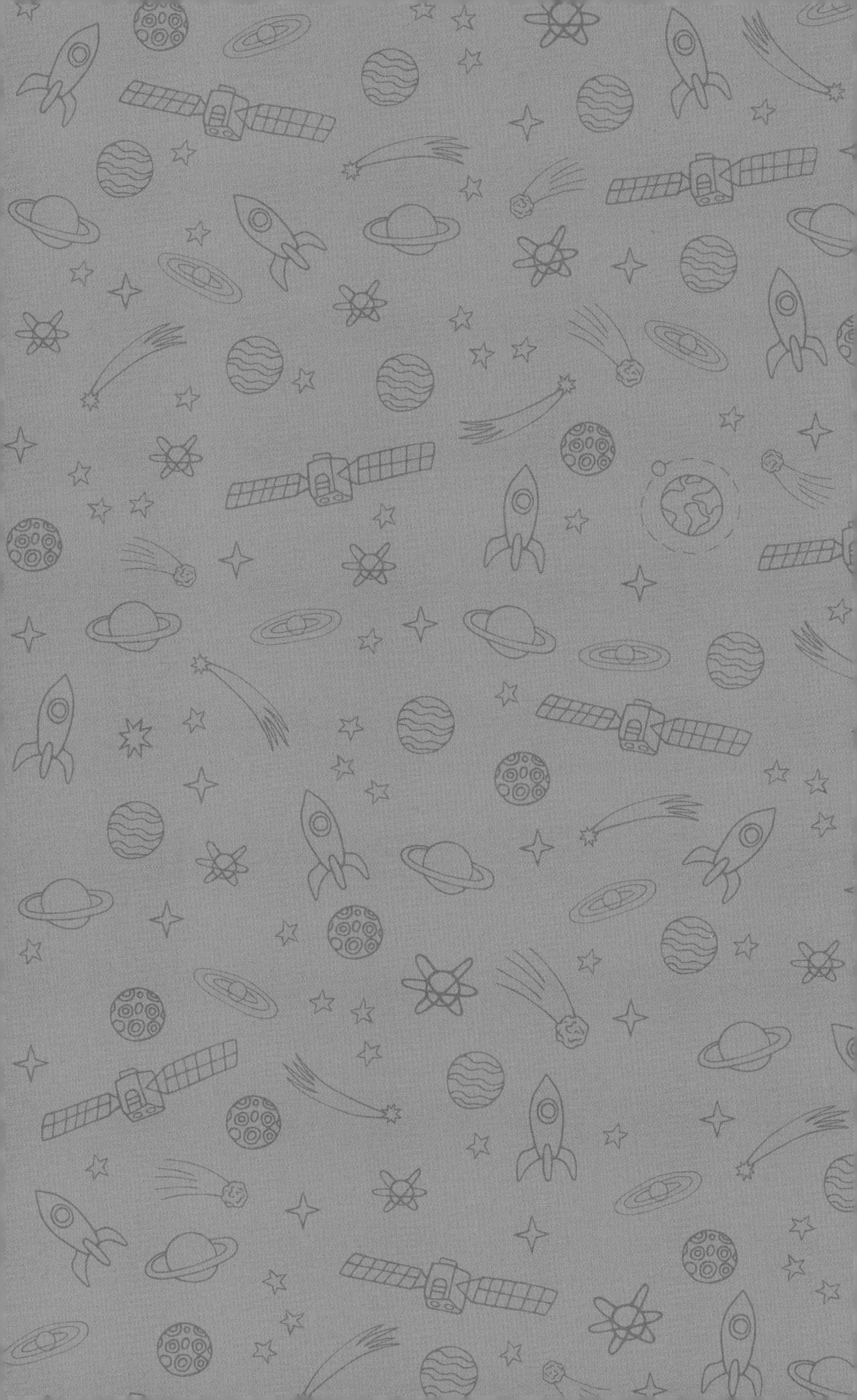

Chapter 1

Mars Looks Cool

Pedro was reading about Mars. He told Miss Winkle, "Mars looks cool. It would be fun to go there."

Katie raised her hand. "I want to go to Saturn. I'll ride around on its rings. I'll get nice and dizzy!"

Miss Winkle said, “You might not like it. The rings of Saturn are made of dust and ice.”

“Yikes!” yelled Katie. “I’ll go somewhere else.”

That night, Pedro told his dad, “I’d like to go to Mars.”

“Are you sure?” asked Pedro’s dad. “It’s far away.”

“That’s okay,” said Pedro. “I have a big suitcase, and I like long trips.”

"Mars is 225 million miles away," said Pedro's dad.

"No problem," said Pedro. "I'll pack lots of sandwiches."

“And bring some cows for milk,” added Pedro’s dad.

That night, Pedro dreamed about going to Mars.

His spaceship was crowded

and noisy. The cows never slept!

Chapter 2

Exploring Planets

The next day, Pedro read more about Mars.

"It's very rocky," said Miss Winkle.

"Great!" Pedro smiled. "I like climbing rocks."

The class read about

Pluto too.

JoJo said, "If I lived on

Pluto, I would see five moons

outside my window."

"Wild!" said Pedro.

Katie told the class, "Saturn has 82 moons."

"No way!" said Pedro.

"It's true," said Miss Winkle. "That sky is very crowded!"

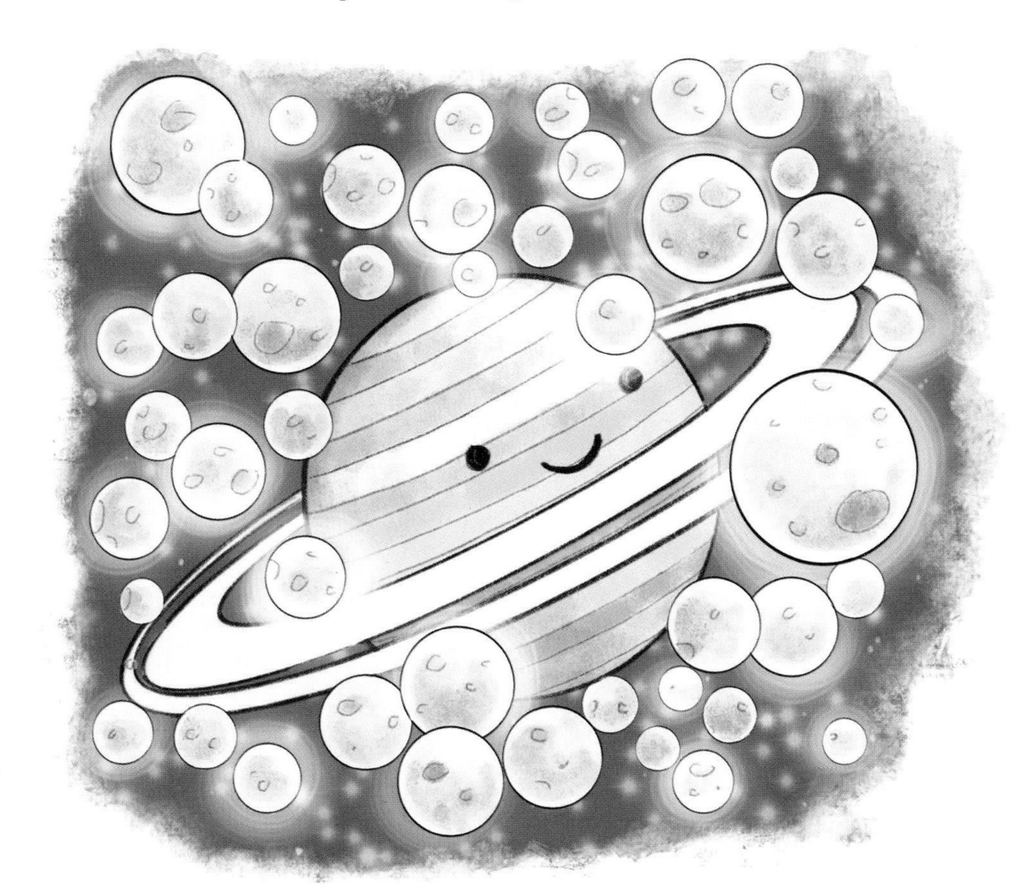

She told the class, “Each of the planets goes around the sun. How many days does it take for Earth to do it?”

Sofia, a new girl, said,

"It takes 365 days."

"Right," said Pedro. "I must wait 365 days for each new birthday. That's a long time."

Later, Pedro asked his dad, "How many days does it take Mars to go around the sun?"

His dad looked it up. "It takes 687 days."

Chapter 3

A Very Nice Planet

The next day, Pedro told Katie, "When I go to Mars, I will have to wait 687 days between birthdays."

"Wow!" said Katie. "That's a long time."

"For sure!" said Pedro.

After school, Pedro and Katie and JoJo played soccer. The sun was shining, and a red cardinal sang a happy song.

Pedro said, “Earth is a very nice planet. I think I’ll stay here for a while.”

“Good idea,” said Katie.

That night, Pedro went

to bed, smiling at the moon.

The moon smiled back!

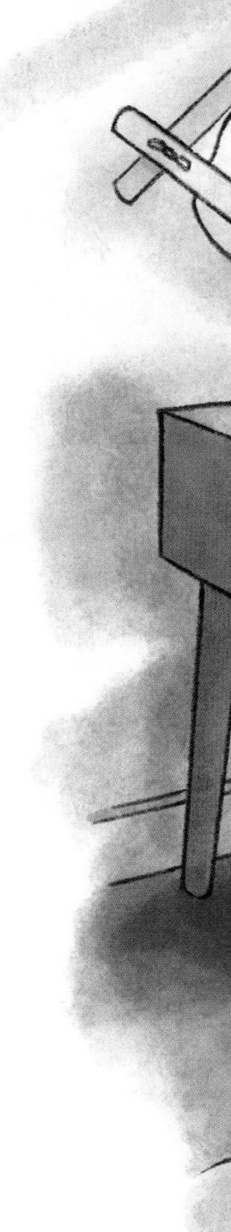

About the Author

Fran Manushkin is the author of Katie Woo, the highly acclaimed fan-favorite early reader series, as well as the popular Pedro series. Her other books include *Happy in Our Skin*, *Baby, Come Out!* and the best-selling board books *Big Girl Panties* and *Big Boy Underpants*. There is a real Katie Woo: Fran's great-niece, but she doesn't get into as much trouble as the Katie in the books. Fran lives in New York City, three blocks from Central Park, where she can often be found bird-watching and daydreaming. She writes at her dining room table, without the help of her naughty cats, Goldy and Chaim.

About the Illustrator

Tammie Lyon began her love for drawing at a young age while sitting at the kitchen table with her dad. She continued her love of art and eventually attended the Columbus College of Art and Design, where she earned a bachelor's degree in fine art. After a brief career as a professional ballet dancer, she decided to devote herself full time to illustration. Today she lives with her husband, Lee, in Cincinnati, Ohio. Her dogs, Gus and Dudley, keep her company as she works in her studio.

Glossary

cardinal (KAR-duh-nuhl)—a songbird with black coloring around the beak and a crest of feathers on its head. The male is bright red.

crowded (KROU-ded)—having a lot of people or items in a small space

dizzy (DIZ-ee)—having a feeling of being unsteady on your feet

noisy (NOI-zee)—loud

planet (PLAN-it)—a large heavenly body that circles the sun

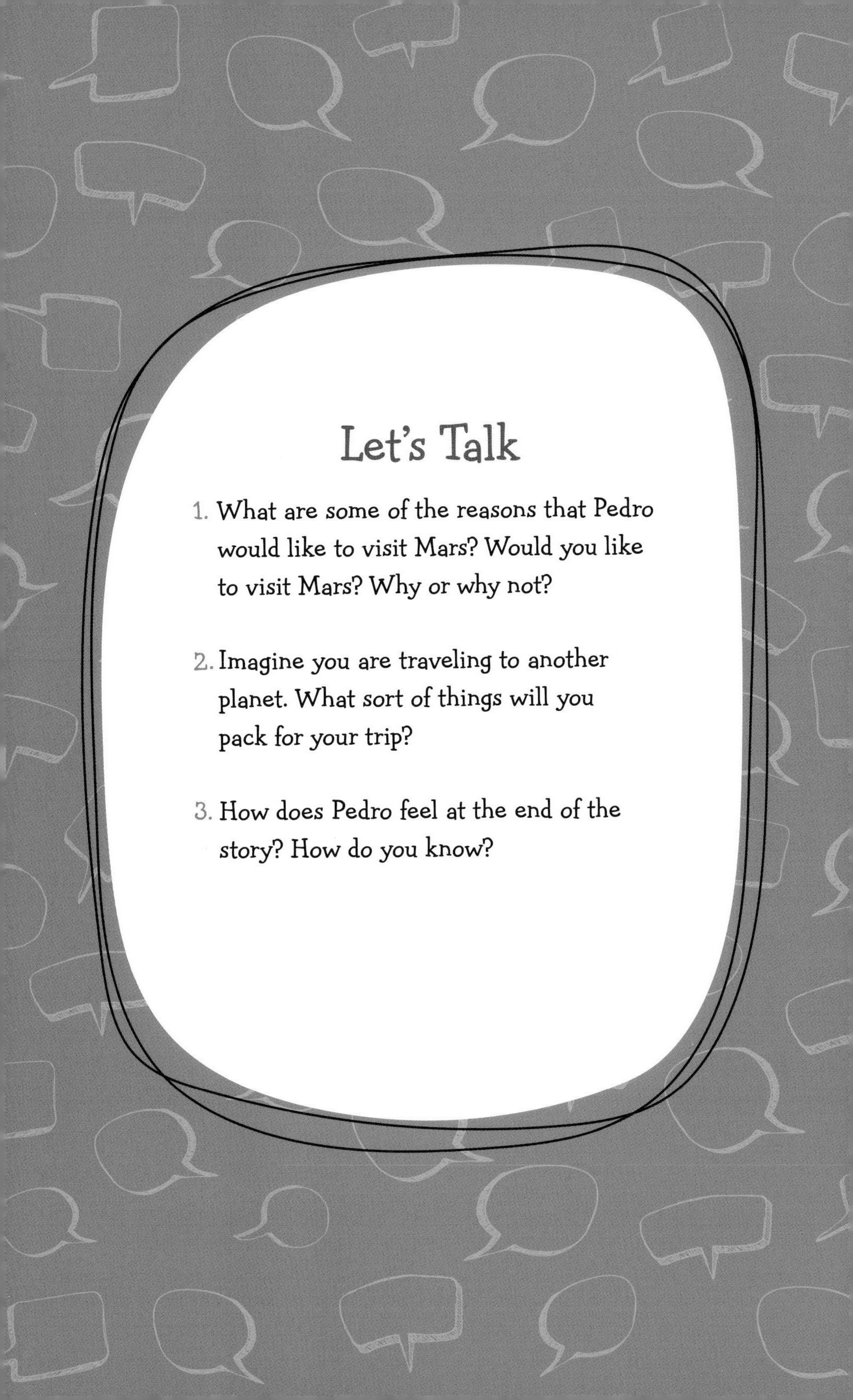

Let's Talk

1. What are some of the reasons that Pedro would like to visit Mars? Would you like to visit Mars? Why or why not?

2. Imagine you are traveling to another planet. What sort of things will you pack for your trip?

3. How does Pedro feel at the end of the story? How do you know?

Let's Write

1. Write a story about traveling in a spaceship with cows.

2. Draw a picture of yourself in outer space. Then write a sentence to describe how you feel to have left Earth.

3. Choose a planet and write down three facts about it. If you don't know three facts, ask a grown-up to help you find some in a book or on the computer.

JOKE AROUND

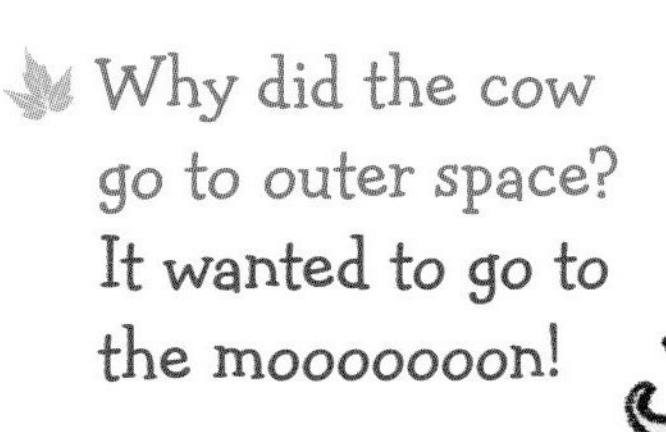

- Why did the cow go to outer space?
  It wanted to go to the mooooooon!

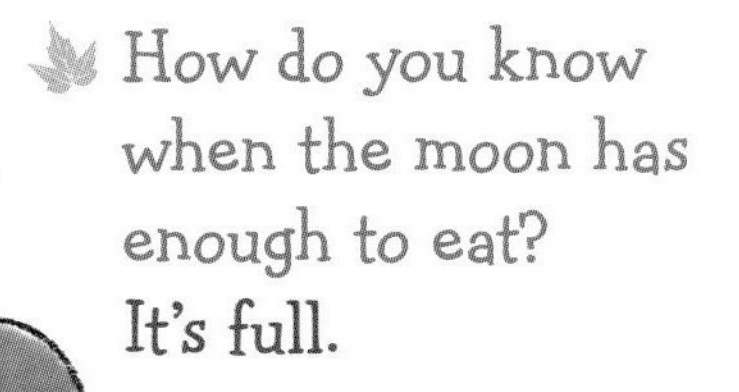

- How do you know when the moon has enough to eat?
  It's full.

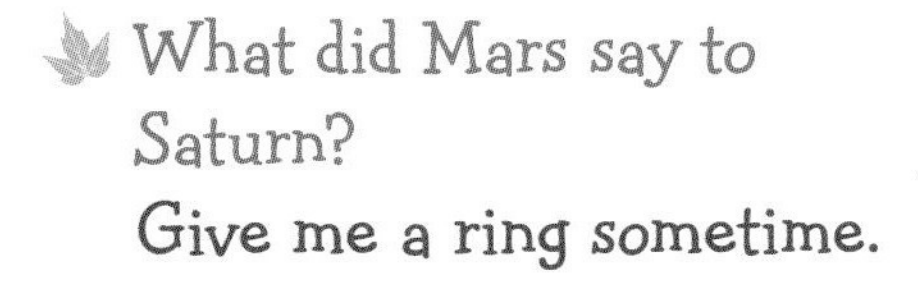

- What did Mars say to Saturn?
  Give me a ring sometime.

- How do you throw a birthday party in space?
  You have to PLAN-et.

What do planets like to read?
Comet books!

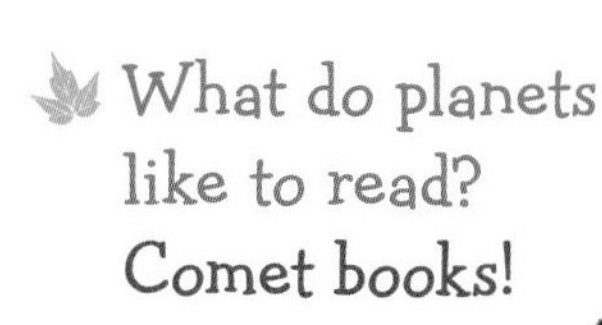

What do planets like to sing?
Nep-tunes

Where did the astronaut keep her sandwiches?
In her launch box

Why didn't the sun go to college?
Because it already had a million degrees!

HAVE MORE FUN WITH PEDRO!